LINDA MCKOWN

PINK SKY IN THE MORNING

Knight Detective Series - Book 2

BY

LINDA MCKOWN

Publisher LindaMcKownAuthor LLC

Scottsdale, AZ

PINK SKY IN THE MORNING

Pink Sky in the Morning

Knight Detective Series – Book 2

ISBN-13: 978-1-7344095-4-3

Library of Congress Control Number: 2021900049

Author:

LindaMcKownAuthor LLC

11574 E Running Deer Trail

Scottsdale, AZ 85262

https://www.lindamckown.com

Front Cover Photo of the book was purchased from Shutterstock. Book title manipulation was done by Joseph McKown

There is a saying Red Sky in the evening, sailor's delight. Red Sky in the morning, sailors take warning. I decided to use Pink as the color to signify the warning. However, bad things do happen anytime in the criminal world. The color of the sky doesn't matter.

Enjoy Book 2 of my new detective series!

Table of Contents

1 Tour Group

The young woman watched as the tanker ship lights drifted further away. The ship was still anchored, and the star on the side of the ship wasn't visible. No one saw her as she undid the lock on the raft, crawled down the metal ladder, and slipped overboard.

The raft drifted away from the tanker. Suddenly, the wind flipped the raft she was on and carried the rubber object out of her reach. She was floating in the cold water and letting the tide push her closer to shore. The time was around midnight.

She removed her gold bracelets and put them in the jacket pocket of her black knit pantsuit. The woman was glad she wore tennis shoes today rather than heels. Her scarf was tied around her long black hair.

"Stupid raft. Now I'll have to swim to shore."

Her small frame wouldn't retain much body heat.

"Below ninety degrees is when you become confused, and your blood vessels constrict."

She turned over and began stroking softly afraid any large splash would attract dangerous fish. There were no sounds from the ship. The woman was safe for the moment, but a night spotter might see the floating raft. She worried and stroked harder toward shore. While swimming her brain was trying to make sense out of her day.

The woman thought about the tour at five o'clock. The others were taken to a blue container on the ship's topside by a worker. There were no letters on the outside but there were numbers on the door. She failed to remember the numbers. He showed the three people the inside of the blue container and played with the temperature control button. She remembered their laughter.

An orange container further away drew her interest. This one contained numbers and the word *Dry*, and she tried to peer inside the slit in the door. Her curiosity about the containers might have saved her. When she turned back, the first container was locked and the people on the tour were gone. There were no voices. The ship worker appeared. She raised her hand to draw his attention. Her mind didn't grasp the situation until she saw a second man. Her hand dropped, and she clutched the container edge.

A masked man had turned the corner and talked to the ship's worker. The worker pointed to the blue container. Her eyes bulged in alarm. That's when she hid under a tarp and didn't move when the tanker left port. Then the ship's engine stopped. She threw away her plastic gloves and the fabric hairnet the worker gave everyone on the tour.

She was afraid for the other people on the tour and afraid of whoever was on the ship that locked them inside. She realized the gloves were to hide their fingerprints, and the netting was to hide hair follicles.

She stopped swimming. The shore looked to be a bit over two hundred yards away. The lights of the houses shown on the crest of the ridge. The woman scanned the shoreline for a dock or building. Her body was getting cold. There wasn't much time.

Suddenly she heard a whirring sound and saw a tiny flash of light. There was a small boat coming from the direction of the tanker. She scanned the water and didn't see anything except the large ship. Pinpoint lights finally appeared.

"The craft must be dark."

She realized the worker might have remembered her. The masked man could have counted the bodies in the container later. Or they saw the raft was missing. He was looking for the mysterious person on the tour. No one asked her name. The woman wanted to scream for help but knew there was no one.

The small craft in the water was moving back and forth in a precise search pattern. The main light flashed her way when the small craft turned. She was glad the raft flipped her out. They motored in the direction the raft floated.

A huge wave shoved her further toward shore. Her scarf vanished. The black hair swirled free. The adrenalin activated. Primal survival and flight mode kicked into high gear. The woman was young and strong. She used her body to surf on the top part of the waves.

The roar of pounding surf reached her ears. She was close. Suddenly she saw a pier jetting out from a small cove. There were about twelve boats moored around the dock. The woman figured the pier was privately-owned. She didn't care.

"Maslow, you were wrong. Safety should be number one and warmth number two on your tower of needs. Those boats represent both to me. You must never have gone swimming in the dark ocean."

The small craft was getting closer. She dove under the water and swam as fast as she could. Finally, she came to the surface for air. The engine noise was louder. Immediately, she sunk under the water and swam toward the dock. She resurfaced and saw there was a ladder from the water to the top.

The woman remembered her gold chain on her right ankle with her initials, *CB*. She forgot about the chain. Something was in the water following her. The approaching watercraft was forgotten. She knew what was in the water was worse. The gold chain was to blame. The object sparkled in the water like a metal lure. The two initial charms added additional luster and intrigue for a fish.

She panicked and started swimming fast toward the ladder. Something slippery touched her leg, and she almost cried out in alarm. The watercraft light flashed her way. She went down underneath the water to hide.

The woman opened her eyes and saw the monster in the water. The dock lights illuminated the small area. She kicked with her feet, barely skimming the sides of the fish.

The ladder was close. Three feet was all she needed. She felt pain in her leg as her hand touched the ladder. The woman yanked with her arms and pulled herself up. The monster jumped after her. She used her strength for a final pull and flew over the ladder. Blood dripped into the water.

The woman looked below her. The small shark viewed through the dock slats was swimming crazily.

"Die, please."

She needed to get off the dock. A dock box blocked her view of the approaching craft. The woman looked around. There were no sailboats.

"Motorboats have faster speed than a sailboat. People don't fall off a motorboat. Smart owners live here. I better hurry."

2 Survival Skills

Lying on the dock, the woman dragged herself toward a thirty-foot white motorboat with a black top and grabbed the dock line. The shark followed under the dock.

"Go away."

The other boat on the left side was more impressive if a person was going fishing.

"Where are the spears when you need one?"

She pulled the fiberglass pleasure craft closer with the line. Rolling herself over the side of the boat, she slid to the boat floor. Crawling toward the door, she pulled. The door opened. The owner was either a trusting soul or forgot to lockup. She was grateful. Hopping down the steps inside the boat, she felt partly safe.

Shore was only steps away. No one was around on the dock, and a dog's throaty bark sounded in the distance.

She grabbed the towels in the head and began ripping the fabric using her teeth. The woman tied the strips around her leg to staunch the bleeding. Then she went outside and wiped the blood upon the boat floor. She hopped back inside and filled a teapot from the stove with cold water.

Going to the top of the boat, she threw the teapot water on the dock to wash away the blood. Hastily moving back inside the boat, she shut the door and turned the door lock. She tried to peek out the small windows.

Fifteen minutes passed. The watercraft bumped against the dock, and the boards creaked from the strain. Her eyes rolled in pain. The leg was swelling once the leg was out of the cold ocean. The woman heard the man's boots hit the dock boards. She didn't see boat lights. He began checking the moored boats one by one. She saw a second person inside the craft near the steering wheel. The man looked like the ship worker.

She stuffed the towel and teapot in the bathroom sink. She quietly closed the bathroom door and hid in the shower. The tiny curtain would have to work. Her tennis shoes squished.

After ten minutes, the man climbed back onto the watercraft, and the small boat motored away. She heaved a sigh of relief. Slowly she stepped out of the head and hopped around the inside of the boat.

Finding a flashlight and first aid kit in a drawer, the curtains were pulled in the bunk bedroom. She sat on the bed and cut a slit in her expensive slacks. She examined her wound. The shark bite wasn't too bad. Her tennis shoe top was ripped off. Her foot was torn, and there was a red crease on her ankle. She would need stitches or tape.

Pouring some antiseptic into the wounds, the woman grabbed tissues to catch the blood and drips. With the scissors, she took squares of non-stick gauze and placed them on top of the leg wound. Finding the half-ripped towel, she cut more strips and rebound the leg. The foot was cleaned, tape strips were cut, and the application of tape pulled the flesh together.

The woman examined the medicine cabinet with her flashlight. There were some expired antibiotic pills which she hoped would do the trick. An infection would be a bad thing. The bottle was stuffed inside her pocket.

The cheap black garbage bag was taken out of the container. She struggled to open the bag. Her wet towels and bandage wrappers were placed inside. Next, a sponge was used to wipe the counter and cupboard surfaces. The floor was scanned for blood drops. She ran the shower for a few minutes to remove the dirt from her shoes.

She rinsed out the soft yellow sponge. The woman didn't know how long she could stay on the boat.

Dropping some ice cubes in a washcloth, she placed the cold on her wound and another on her foot to reduce the swelling. The rest were put in a glass of water. She took a drink. The ice packs were set aside after a few minutes. She shivered and goosebumps rose on her arms.

The drawers in the main bedroom were checked, and a small wool buffalo-check blanket was taken out. The young woman found some knit slacks and a cotton shirt. Stripping out of her wet clothes, she stood naked for a couple of minutes. The boat rocked, and she felt dizzy. Grabbing the dry clothes off the bed, she quickly changed. Limping, she crept outside and found a wood stick onshore.

The woman moved slowly toward the dock gate and read the large white sign. There were scroll letters in red and black with a crest. She knew which neighborhood she landed.

"Pacific Crest Estates are exclusive."

For the moment, the woman was content to be alive.

"Rich people live here. A person can't ever get away from them."

3 Naïve Decision

She scanned the shoreline and decided walking was out of the question. Her leg wouldn't make the journey over sand and high cliffs. She could see large rocks in the other direction. Climbing the rocks was out of the question.

The black-haired young woman went back to the large white pleasure boat. There was no gun onboard. The ship to shore radio stood in a corner. The passcode was taped to the receiver. The young woman paused in her movements.

"Trust is difficult. Who should I tell? They will ask too many questions. I'll be blamed."

Although hurt and confused, she made her call. There was no answer.

She was going to dial a different number, and she remembered their last fight.

"My nemesis harped over and over, what do you wish to accomplish? How do I know? I am sick of her. She never shuts up."

The young woman grabbed more towels to put on her wounds. She lowered the table. Cushions were placed under her leg. The ice packs were added. The blanket was warm and cuddly. She slowly chewed the pills, took a sip of water, and crashed until morning. The stick was her only weapon. Her eyes closed, and the woman drifted asleep.

Awakening with a jerk, her body was numb. She looked out the window at the early morning light and the water around the dock. The shark was floating. She yawned. The shark's body was almost severed in two.

"There is justice in this world. The watercraft must have caught the tail."

The woman hobbled out to look at the shark's mouth. A piece of seaweed floated over the head. The seaweed floated away while she looked across the water from the boat. There was no large tanker ship. She wondered if the nightmare was real or not.

Her leg hurt. The woman knew something bad happened. The tanker was real. She looked at the dead shark. Her ankle bracelet was stuck in the teeth. She stepped on the dock, opened a bin, and found a short paddle. She opened the boat's back fiberglass door and stood on the back portion of the boat. The tide was carrying the dead fish further from the dock. She leaned out as far as she could reach. Her initials gleamed in the sunlight.

The woman thought about starting the motor manually. Stealing a boat would be bad news. This was not the time.

"There goes three hundred dollars plus fifty more for the initials. At least I didn't buy the initials with diamonds."

She noticed the name on the back end of the white yacht. The black lettering shouted at her.

Charm School.

"This is unbelievable."

She raised her fist in the air in defiance. The woman's anger almost dissipated. She put the oar away. Slamming the bin lid in disgust, she returned to the pleasure boat. The bin was the perfect solution to dump her troubles. She was lucky no one saw or heard her.

"I was almost shark bait and lost my favorite piece of jewelry."

The woman angrily tried the phone number again. She was chewing on salty crackers and canned tuna found in the cupboard. The woman hung up.

"Where is he? Breathe slowly and think before you leap."

She knew somehow her life was in trouble. The woman worried about some of her decisions. The consequences were high. Her stubbornness was to blame.

Looking out the boat window she saw a man walk his large dog. Although the area appeared peaceful, there was danger. She couldn't stay in the white and black boat forever. The owner would take the pleasure craft out for a ride. She touched the white square and the black square of the fabric. In between the squares was the gray color. She was getting too absorbed in ridiculous thoughts.

Letting the black and white checked curtain go, she went and sat next to the radio. Her hand hesitated a second time. Maybe her brain was trying to tell her something.

She noticed the blood seeping through her foot. The flexible tape came loose. After changing her bandages and taking more pills, she tried the phone again.

The man finally answered. He sounded out of breath.

The woman was relieved to hear a voice. She no longer was alone in this mess. Telling her friend where she was located and what happened, he understood. The man would be there soon.

"Cathy, hold on, and stay put. I'll find you and I might take an hour to drive there. This is a dangerous turn of events."

"You sound winded."

The man hesitated. He couldn't explain. There was a moment of shock that enveloped him when he received her call and heard her story.

"I didn't know you went on the tour. You saw a masked person on the ship. There's a shocker. They do wear plastic shield masks when they are around the chemical containers. If they don't, the boss will fire them."

"Be quiet."

Cathy put her hand over the microphone. One of the boats on the dock took off. She saw the fishing boat leave. She uncovered the device.

"I'm back. The face mask wasn't the chemical ones. I know the difference. Paul is in shipping unless you've forgotten."

The man would need to handle the new development. A hysterical reaction never solved anything.

"The mask didn't look like a chemical mask. Okay, calm down. I heard. You did see another ship worker near a container. His face is etched in your brain. This worker made people disappear. You somehow hid in fear and swam to shore. We'll talk later. I'll need to figure out how to fix things."

"Why do you have to fix things? All I need is a ride and some minor help getting medicine."

He was becoming irritated by her questions.

"I have to convince the guard gate to let me in the housing area where this pleasure boat is moored."

"I might need stitches."

He shook his head in disgust. The man tried to control his voice.

"I'll make a call."

Visibly disturbed by the turn of events, the man grabbed his car keys and left. He mumbled to himself.

"The naïve mouse hid from the cat. Great!"

4 Australia

The water was pleasurable and warm. She floated when something bumped her. The young woman lazily smiled.

"Hey, we should get out of the pool. I told you the pink sky this morning wasn't good. There's a storm brewing."

Penelope Knight looked at her dark-haired husband with brown eyes. His face was close and tanned. Her blonde hair floated in the water, and her brown eyes stared at his muscular body. She liked his body.

"Aren't there ancient weather sayings about a red sky? I don't remember a pink anything in the warning."

"Pink is pale red like the color in your swimsuit," said Liam.

He liked seeing her tanned shapely body and the spaces that weren't tan. He moved her strap a little and kissed the spot. He kissed a little lower.

Penelope looked at her husband on the white foam float. They were in the hotel pool after their surfing lesson around Byron Bay, Australia.

"Did I tell you today how gorgeous you look?"

"Ten times aren't enough. Tell me more and stop moving my straps back and forth."

He pushed her float in the ladder direction.

"My fair maiden, come back to me."

She could feel the wind, and the upper sky was changing into darkness with massive clouds. The air felt cool, and her body shivered. He paddled closer.

"This fair maiden believes her knight about an impending storm."

His wife slid into the water. He did the same and shoved the floats. They swam to the pool's metal ladder and climbed out. Liam grabbed the stray floats and handed them to the pool attendant. With their towels and sandals in their hands, they ran inside the hotel.

Walking through the lobby, he opened the door to their room. Liam turned on the music to a low volume. He was the first to take a shower. He was done in five minutes, and Penelope touched the white tile soap dish to make sure there was a second soap bar. She took her shower. When she came out, Liam was on the phone ordering their dinner.

"We're having good old-fashioned chicken soup with bread and a fruit basket."

"Thank you. I hate to say this, but I'm tired of eating out."

Penelope sat on the edge of their bed in a soft sarong outfit. Liam wore casual knit shorts and a top.

"We've had five days here not counting the nine days at my parent's place in Montana doing the wedding thing."

"Our wedding was more than a thing. It was the best party ever."

Penelope was glad they didn't elope.

"We should pack after we eat."

Liam hated packing.

"Our flight leaves early for Sydney. We have a couple of hours in Sydney before we fly to Los Angeles. There is another stop in between."

"I'm all right with the layover and stops. You never know if our flights will arrive on time," mentioned Penelope.

Liam didn't like flying in bad weather. "Let's hope this storm doesn't delay our takeoff. I'm worried that we won't make the Fiji flight."

"We will make Fiji. I'm positive the weather forecast said clear for Sydney."

The food cart arrived and was brought inside their room. Liam gave the man a tip, and they sat down at the small table to eat. Both were tired from their honeymoon and the vigorous exercise of four days of surfing. They ate in silence. Liam parked the trays outside their door. He saved some bread and fruit for the morning.

Sitting on the couch, they listened to the weather. Liam put his arm around his new wife.

"I love you, detective wife."

Penelope was happy and pleased. The honeymoon was a success from beginning to end.

"Hold me close."

He put both arms around her. Penelope spoke.

"I feel the same. I wish we had a few more days off. Going back to work doesn't seem so exciting."

Liam felt the opposite. He was pleased to return to his detective job. The next case was always waiting. He was the department's lead detective. Penelope would join him as one of the groups of detectives in his team. Her skills would help in the investigation.

"At least we get to work together again. I'm looking forward to riding in a company car with you."

"Dedication has always been your mantra," mentioned his wife.

"Thank you, Very nicely stated. I suppose the office will have to start calling you Detective Knight."

During their break on the beach, he called Hugh Farris, a detective already on the current multiple murder case.

"What did Hugh have to say? I saw you try to hide your cell phone from the surfing instructor."

"The arson fire at the warehouse in Los Angeles started from explosives placed near the exits. They still haven't found the security guards nor have the guards reported to the owner. The drug enforcement group thought besides a drug lab, some other items were being shipped there illegally. The stolen drones from a prior burglary the month before at a different warehouse might have been the start. The police have arrested the owner of the warehouses."

Penelope thought about the case.

"I thought the insurance company paid for the loss of the drones. There were serial numbers reported. I don't understand; the owner didn't know about the drug lab on his property."

Liam rubbed his face.

"I know he didn't, but he should have checked his warehouses on occasion. The police want to blame someone for the six deaths."

"Any identification yet on those six people? We assume they died from smoke inhalation."

"Not yet. Hugh asked my friend who owns a restaurant in downtown Los Angeles for street information."

"I remember Dugan. He's like a rich snitch. What did he have to say?"

"Dugan told Hugh no one on the street was talking, or else they didn't know anything. Dugan did find a man who mentioned the Beeker Star Ships Company commander. The original commander was James Beeker."

Penelope knew who James Beeker was in the business world. He owned a huge shipping fleet that shipped containers of goods on tanker ships. He was a self-made billionaire. All his ships contained the Star symbol somewhere on the side of the tanker, and the names were Star something or other.

"I thought James Beeker died a few years ago."

"He did. His son, Paul Beeker, has owned the fleet for three years. He moved to Los Angeles about a year ago from New York. He met his wife on a trip to Hong Kong seven years earlier. They currently live in a plush mansion with huge garages and grounds in Los Angeles."

Penelope blinked in recognition. She remembered reading the article in the magazine showcasing the opulent home.

"Her name is Jane Beeker. She has a younger sister. Both women have dark hair and are beautifully exotic."

Liam was impressed.

"You are correct. There is a billion-dollar question. Why would James or his son ever become involved in a drug lab? James Beeker was a straight shooter. He took pride in his business."

Penelope stood.

"We should start packing. Maybe the son doesn't believe in the same things his father did."

"Paul was a playboy for a long time. However, I think he has changed. He hasn't aroused any suspicions with the police or shipping community in his three-year reign as CEO."

Liam stood and grabbed Penelope's soft hand. Her wedding ring sparkled. The diamond was large.

"Enough about the case, why don't I set the alarm, and we can pack in the morning. I have a better idea of what to do with the rest of our honeymoon time."

Penelope knew that look in his eyes. The look she saw when they first met was one of surprise and instant massive like. She kissed her husband, and they disappeared into their bedroom. Packing would only take fifteen minutes in the morning.

Liam took his wife in his arms.

"You always feel exceptionally wonderful. Since I met you, my life has changed for the better."

"No more playboy."

"No more being alone and single. My heart beats faster whenever you are around. Then there's your touch."

She sighed blissfully.

"We're really good together. The nights are the best, my love. We don't need the moonlight to spin out of control."

He returned her kisses.

"I like the moonlight. The view is better."

The gray rain began pummeling the hotel roof. The water ran down the patio door and formed a gulley in the street. Waves crashed onto the beaches spewing seaweed onto the shore. They could hear shutters banging below them.

The two people didn't care. They were in love, and their hearts were currently touching. Sparks were always necessary. The lightning lit the sky.

5 Monday Afternoon

Captain Jonathan Harrison of the Los Angeles Detective Department looked at his two detectives. He enjoyed seeing them because they looked rested and well. Hugh walked into the afternoon meeting with his homemade cup. Coffee stains were on the side.

"Hello, the newlyweds have returned to the big city. You look beautifully tanned Penelope. I bet your partner played outside the whole time under a broken umbrella. Or was the object a surfboard? His nose is peeling."

Liam touched his nose.

"Gotcha!"

"Hugh, the coffee grounds are gone from my office," answered Liam.

Penelope chuckled. Her husband was annoyed, and they were in the office for only five minutes.

Hugh handed over one new bag and an opened bag of coffee.

"Notice how I bought the good kind that I enjoy. There might be a cup of coffee missing from the other bag. You were late."

The two detectives slept in because their airplane left Fiji later than planned due to bad weather. The Captain knew about their delay and moved the start time of the meeting for them. Detectives Carter and Davidson joined them in the boss's office. Carter sheepishly handed over a bag of coffee to Liam.

"The coffee shop only carried the whole beans."

The Captain pulled a small electric grinder out of his drawer.

"Now that all my detectives are in one spot and we have the missing coffee fund, I'll let Hugh take the lead in describing our recent findings. I have missed our meetings. I'm going to try to make more of them."

Hugh stood and went to the whiteboard and added to the already laid out diagrams of the crime story.

"Six people died in an arson fire at a large warehouse complex in Los Angeles. The owner was arrested and released when the police found out he leased the building to a corporation that has vanished. The drug guys are working the lab found at the warehouse. They will keep us updated. Two security guards were missing. We have identified the two men as Mr. Hector and Mr. Hernandez who are two of the victims that died of smoke inhalation."

Hugh paused. Liam frowned.

"What about the other four victims?"

Hugh pulled out a sheet of paper and handed it to Liam. Liam read the coroner's report.

"Four of the victims died from hypothermia. Three of them showed the same approximate time of death. The fourth victim died twelve to fifteen hours later. This can't be correct. Is there even snow on our state's mountains?"

Hugh nodded.

"The report is correct. None of us saw this one. The coroner was thorough when he finally got to our little group of bodies. We will need to find the refrigeration or freezer unit. There isn't any at the warehouse involved."

Penelope still hadn't heard the names of the victims which meant they didn't know the identities.

"Has anyone reported people missing from their place of business? I would think after two weeks that employers might recognize employees are gone longer than usual. Some of these four people knew neighbors or relatives," said Penelope.

Liam handed the report back to Hugh.

"I'll want all the information we have accumulated on my desk, so I can follow through with my report at the end of this week. Now that Penelope and I are back, Davidson and Carter can take a break. I do need you to be available if we decide to do a stakeout."

Davidson and Carter nodded. Jonathan dismissed them from the meeting.

"A friend of mine owns a boat at the Pacific Crest Estates. He thought his cruiser was broken into recently. There was nothing taken that he could see except his first aid kit was empty. I told him to submit the report to the police and to lock his boat in the future."

Liam knew his Captain's friend should be more careful. People did steal cruisers on occasion. Jonathan handed a call record to Liam.

"As the lead detective, I'll let you take care of this call that came in this morning. We're glad to have you both back."

Their Captain dismissed Liam and Penelope who went into Liam's new office. Liam put the coffee away except for the open bag. Penelope made coffee while Liam read the call record.

His wife handed him a cup of freshly brewed coffee and poured a cup for herself. She sat down in a chair across from him and took a sip.

Liam automatically grabbed the coffee and stirred in the packet of sugar.

"There is nothing yet on the identities. We might have a small piece to work with today. Would you like to meet Paul Beeker?"

Penelope looked surprised. He handed her the call log.

She read, "Mr. Beeker believes his ship, Star Caroline II, has a container that has been tampered with approximately two weeks ago. The tanker has reached a dock in Mexico. Why would he report the problem to us versus the Mexican authorities?"

"The ship is registered here and was inspected here. He has also reported the problem to Logistics Inspection in Los Angeles. They will have the Mexican authorities check the container contents per the manifest."

Liam made the phone call to Paul Beeker, and they were scheduled to meet him at another ship at a loading dock in Los Angeles.

"We should ask him if he is missing any employees."

Liam smiled.

"My thoughts and yours run along the same vein. This meeting should be interesting. I wonder how much Paul knows about his shipping business."

Penelope finished her coffee.

"I'll get us some egg salad sandwiches from the deli with Hugh's help. Do you want Hugh to go with us to the interview this afternoon?"

Liam thought about whether they should bring Hugh.

"I think two detectives would be considered normal. Three detectives might look like trouble and come off as suspicious. Let Hugh know about the upcoming meeting."

Penelope left her husband's office to find Hugh. Liam went to his computer to do some research regarding Paul Beeker and his father. Then he turned to Beeker's wife Jane.

"Jane was a singer in Hong Kong at a small-time bar. This is an unusual coupling between a rich man's son and a middle-class female. Hong Kong seems like an odd place for vacation. None of his ships travel there, and most people have been vacationing to Dubai."

Penelope came back with a bag of egg salad sandwiches and chips. Hugh sat with the two detectives eating a late lunch.

"They cooked these eggs exactly right. They are delicious with the sweet pickle and thousand island dressing. About the Beeker family, promise me if Mr. Beeker has a party, you will wiggle my wife, Emma, and me an invitation. My wife would kill to see the Beeker mansion. I bet their chef can make these egg salad sandwiches. He probably cuts off the crust, triple stacks the slices, and feeds the crusts to his organic-fed chickens when he arrives home."

Liam laughed.

"Same old Hugh. Food is first, party mansions second, and lastly, there's the chef and more food. Nothing has changed. The word party does mean fun for the Beeker mansion. I suppose we should also request invites for Dodge and his dog."

"No, don't bring the dog!" said Hugh.

Penelope looked at the two men.

"The dog knows how to smell out drugs."

Liam shook his head.

"The only thing on the premises will be lots of Tequila. They usually serve the three hundred and fifty-dollar bottles. Although the bar does have some two thousand five hundred dollar bottles the last time I was there. The cellar has priceless stuff."

Hugh perked up.

"A cellar in their basement contains the good stuff. You've been to the mansion and the cellar. When did you go there?"

"Becka, my old designer girlfriend, was invited by one of her clients. I tagged along. The cellar is about eight hundred fifty square feet."

Penelope stopped eating her egg sandwich. She put the last three bites down on Liam's desk. He grabbed the rest of her sandwich. Mentioning Becka was a sore point with Penelope. Hugh rattled on as if nothing happened. She looked away.

"So, you know Paul Beeker."

"Yes, I have met him at a party besides the cellar. We were also going to meet Paul and Jane in Greece. I bowed out of the dinner to talk with our boss, Jonathan, about Mrs. Hicks's murder case," said Liam.

"Goodie, I can hardly wait to hear about your interview with Mr. Beeker when you return. Goodbye, kiddies."

Hugh left the office.

"Sorry about talking about Becka but you needed to know. Her name may come up in our interview. I didn't want you to be blindsided. Paul may not know we married. We aren't shipping news."

Penelope stood.

"I'm fine. I have some work to do until later this afternoon."

His wife left his office. Liam knew she was upset with him. It wasn't the way she walked or talked. There was a feeling of estrangement because she didn't smile at him. She always smiled at him before leaving his office.

The interview would need to be carefully worded to not upset Beeker or Penelope. Liam wondered if putting Penelope on the case was a good idea. Much as he and Hugh disagreed with each other, the other older detective might have been a better choice.

He thought about Dodge Riskin, a retired LA detective the department used in the past. Calling Dodge to see if he was not busy, he wondered about the warehouse. They might need an outsider to monitor the warehouse or shipyard activity. He didn't like the cause of the deaths of any of the victims.

Liam went to see his Captain. He let him know the interview time was set. He wanted to pull Penelope from the interview.

Jonathan looked at Liam skeptically.

"You and Penelope will make an excellent cover. You know the Beeker family better than anyone. With your newbie wife in tow, he might drop his guard. The man likes beautiful. Detectives are no exception."

Liam was going to protest, but he knew his Captain was correct. Penelope also saw things men missed, and she could keep a conversation going at great length no matter their status in life. He grudgingly agreed, she would be an asset.

"Call me this evening if anything changes."

"Yes, sir."

Liam came out of Jonathan's office, and Penelope wasn't at her desk. He didn't appreciate her disappearance.

6 Paul Beeker

The maid led the two detectives into a room filled with volumes of books. The shelves were clean of any dust. Penelope looked inside some of the books while they waited. She was glad Paul changed the date and location of their meeting. A person's home usually revealed a lot about a person. Many of the books were about ships, shipping laws, and various commodities worthy of shipping across distances.

She looked at the pictures on the walls. They were oil paintings of tankers new and old. One picture was a tanker stranded and lying on its side. The tanker's name was Star Caroline.

"This ship came to a bad end. Did you notice the name, Liam?"

Liam stood on the red rug and looked at the picture. He noticed a tiny signature and date in the corner. Paul suddenly appeared in the room.

"The original Star Caroline was my father's first freighter. He kept her in service for too long. She ran into a rogue hurricane. The entire shipment was lost and most of the crew. My father paid dearly for that ship. Love is a fickle thing. Hello, Liam. Who is your friend?"

Liam turned around and shook hands with Paul.

"This is Detective Penelope Knight, my wife."

Paul stood still and gave the female detective a once over. He realized the reason Liam wasn't at dinner in Greece. He recovered nicely.

"Mrs. Knight, this is a pleasure. I'm sorry for the last-minute change to this meeting."

She extended her hand.

"You can call me Penelope. Detective Knight seems a little too formal when I'm in your home with my husband. The library is wonderful."

"Thank you."

Liam sat down as did his detective. Paul sat down at the large desk and pulled out a document.

"Here is the report my firm has submitted to our insurance. The tanker, Star Caroline II, was inspected and cleared to leave port from Los Angeles. Upon reaching three miles out, the ship encountered engine problems. It took eighteen minutes for the tanker to stop forward motion. My captain, Kale Dunkin, anchored the ship and assessed the situation. The damaged part was removed. A helicopter flew him and our engineer to the harbor. They took the part to our repair center. The senior officer was left in charge around ten o'clock in the evening. The senior officer and some of the crew stayed in the engine room to see if there were any other problems. After four hours, my captain and engineer flew back to the tanker, reinstalled the gear part, pulled anchor, and left."

Liam looked at Penelope.

"Did the senior officer see anything unusual?" asked Penelope.

"Yes, Juan Hermosa did before they went below. There were some sharks in the area. The rest of the dockworkers went to bed because morning comes early for them to start checking the containers. A few men were posted to watch."

Liam wondered about the anchored ship. This seemed highly unusual once a ship was cleared to leave port.

"Shouldn't the ship have gone through a reinspection and the certificate reissued?"

Paul hesitated.

"Normally, I would agree with you. We anchored instead and didn't use expensive tugs to return to port. I take full responsibility and probably shouldn't have mentioned our engine problem. With us being friends, I decided to speak, frankly."

Liam felt like a pawn in some game. Paul was curiously watching his wife. This was not a good thing. Liam was protective regarding her. Penelope lowered her leg and smoothed her skirt. She rested her hands on her knees. She felt Liam's restrained manner.

Struggling for words, Liam broke the uncomfortable silence, "I assume the container with the broken lock was above ship which means the containers were lashed with bars or turnbuckles."

Paul pulled himself away from his assessment of the other man's wife.

"Liam, I am impressed. This ship has a normal section on top and room for some specialty containers. The specialty containers aren't the standard twenty feet. They are ten feet each and we put two together. In the lower hold, we have some allowance for the forty-foot containers which can also accommodate two of the twenty footers with mid-locks. Those lower containers are locked in place with cell guides. The turnbuckles are used on the upper three levels, otherwise, the containers are lashed to secure them."

Liam wasn't sure about the top short containers.

"Getting back to the specialty containers, what type of products would be contained in them?"

"We have a refrigerated blue container to ship the tequila bottles to keep them at a constant temperature. There are other containers for shipping lighter weight and more important cargo. On the top containers, we use permanent twist locks that are manual. Any ship deckhand would know how to unlock the device."

Liam asked the capacity of the ship.

"She is one of our smaller ships and carries six thousand eighty-six TEU's or containers. Because we have various sizes and do ship for some other companies, the ship can take as long as four days to unload. Once cleared, they unloaded in two days."

Penelope looked toward Liam and decided to ask the next question.

"Are all the members of your crew accounted for on the ship?"

Paul immediately answered.

"Yes. Some of them have left the ship and will return once we start reloading. Quite a few have families in Mexico."

Liam took over the interview.

"No items were missing from the container that was broken into on the ship?"

"The ship's crew counted the meat products, and no items were missing from the refrigeration unit. We do ship meat back to Mexico. None of the seals on the locked boxes were broken. All the other shipping containers were locked and showed no signs of illegal tampering. We might have taken on a stowaway in Los Angeles that caused the damage and decided to jump ship, or the possibility is a disgruntled worker. We've had issues in the past," commented Paul.

"Wouldn't they need a boat to get off your ship?"

"A small watercraft could have rolled alongside the ship. Thieves on the water are quiet. A small navy-colored boat is hard to see if they turn off the lights. We did lose a raft, but the wind might have caught it during travel. The locks on the rafts aren't problem-free and have popped open. We are purchasing better rafts with sounder locks for our ships."

Liam stood and walked over to Paul. Penelope stood.

"We will submit your report to the police. They may want to talk to your captain on the tanker, the engineer, and the officer. In the meantime, I would recommend staying close to home. Let me know when the ship has returned from Mexico to the port in Los Angeles."

Paul opened the library door for their departure.

"I will. Let's hope there are no more incidents on any of my ships. If something further develops, I will contact your office. Maybe we can chat more in the future. My wife likes to throw parties on occasion. I'm about ready for a break from work. Good day, Liam and Penelope."

On the drive back to the office, he pulled over and looked at his wife.

"The man doesn't know what happened on his ship, or he is a very good liar."

"I agree. He knows something went wrong."

Penelope waited for Liam to pull onto the road. She looked at him questioningly. He asked quietly, "Are we good?"

"About this morning, I think I am all right. There was a momentary flashback to an anti-social encounter with Becka."

Liam took her hand. He squeezed her fingers.

"I'm glad because we need to work on this case. There are feelings things might go wrong. The broken lock on a refrigeration container has aroused my suspicious nature. Paul Beeker hasn't changed much since the last time I saw him."

Penelope worried.

"You think someone is targeting Paul Beeker?"

Liam wasn't sure. His wife pulled him back from the interview episode. He became the lead detective again in a difficult case. One of his detectives pointed out another possibility.

"There is always the possibility that the Beeker company is a target."

He relinquished her hand and drove to the office.

7 Missing Persons

Another week went by with no leads on the identities of the four bodies. Liam and Hugh were getting frustrated. They walked to the deli. The day was warm, and the cement attracted the birds near the water sprinklers. The flow of water made the bugs come out of the dirt. Hugh's short legs were working overtime to keep up with Liam. He stepped over the water.

"Slow down. My loafers are getting wet."

Liam saw Hugh's loafers. His shoes were also wet, but the extra wax made the water droplets stand up. He stomped his feet, turned, and walked some steps into the small shop. Other tables outside were beginning to fill with office workers.

"I'm glad we are doing lunch. Where's Penelope?"

Liam ordered for both. There was no deviation from their sandwich preferences. The deli made the sandwiches the same size and delicious meat for the last ten years. The slices were thick. The cost rose but the customers didn't mind.

"She is at the hairdresser during her lunch break getting a quick trim. Hugh, your hair looks thinner, and you should exercise more."

He handed the sandwich to his friend as they grabbed a nearby table. Hugh put mustard on his ham sandwich, and Liam put horseradish on his beef sandwich.

"I called Dodge to see if he was busy."

Hugh ate a large bite, stopped, and opened the wheat bun.

"How's his helicopter? My exercise machine at home broke."

Liam grinned.

"He said to tell you the bird is working great. He has a friend who owns an airplane, and the man bought some floats. They have been practicing landing and takeoff."

"He should try some troll fishing when he skims over the water."

Liam chuckled at the image of a pilot trying to fish with an airplane.

"Isn't it illegal to snag the fish?"

Hugh looked at the meat in his sandwich and squeezed on the second packet of mustard. He was satisfied when the mustard oozed a little upon the second bite. He grabbed a napkin just in case. The white and gray striped shirt he was wearing was new.

"I don't know. I never went fishing before."

Liam finished his sandwich.

"Seriously? There is a huge ocean right out your front door."

Hugh put his sandwich down.

"Look, some of us didn't have a dad to show us cool stuff. My mom bought the fish at the meat market. I believed fish came in white paper with no heads or insides. Usually, she bought the skinned fish."

The lead detective shook his head. His mind rolled over the number of times he went fishing. He could remember at least twelve worthwhile trips. Never fishing must be some sort of crime. An idea began forming.

"We should go camping together and try some fishing. Fishing a quiet lake would be a good place to start. Beginners always do lakes. The lake should contain bass or trout which means we go North. Those fish are a perfect size. I can help you select your gear and show you how to clean the fish."

Hugh pondered camping in a tent with Dodge and Liam.

"As long as I get to pick where I sleep, I'll go. The doorway is where the bears come inside. I'd rather they eat either you or Dodge. Or better yet, we take two tents. My wife told me sometimes I snore."

Liam knew Hugh was cured of the doldrums. He was back to being cranky.

"Who do you think the four people might be? They must have worked here before. Per the coroner, they were dressed in the casual dress which says to me a professional worker."

Hugh finished his sandwich and threw their garbage in the trash.

"You asked Mr. Beeker about his crew on Star Caroline II. Did you ask him about any of his other ships, dock workers, or his office personnel?"

"We didn't. If someone were missing, he would have told us. I'm assuming of course. The interview only revealed the insurance report and his father's love for an old ship."

Liam answered his telephone. Hugh couldn't read his face. Liam wrote something down in his small notebook. He disconnected from the call.

"What has happened?"

"Our Captain received a call from Mr. Beeker. Paul's wife, Jane, has returned from a three-week spa vacation in the Caribbean. She is head of the Human Resources Department of their company. Four employees were to return from their two-week vacation on Monday. None of them have shown up at their jobs. She wants to report them as missing. Paul thought she was being overwrought but called anyway. She can't report them as missing until tomorrow when the twenty-four hours have expired. She did call their relatives and found some information. Three people never appeared at their vacation hotel in Oregon. The other parent didn't know if their son took a vacation or not."

Hugh looked at the four names Liam wrote down. He read the names out loud.

"Blake and Melody Barkley, chemical and electrical scientists; Simon Needham, avionics; and Karry Sullivan, a software engineer. These people sound important and are probably paid a good salary."

They left the deli and returned to the office.

"Have the police run their names through our databases. I have a feeling we aren't talking citizens of the United States. They might be here on Visas."

Hugh disappeared.

Penelope walked into her husband's office.

"Your hair looks nice down. You should wear it long at work. I'm the only one who gets to see your hair."

He kissed her.

"People in the office will see us."

"I don't mind. They can go find their babe on their own time."

Her eyes twinkled, and he was happy. The new yellow and navy suit she was wearing accented her hair. She also bought him navy slacks and a white shirt for the office. He appreciated her taking the time to find him clothes. Appearances were important in their job.

"Where did Hugh rush off?"

Liam motioned to the chair.

"We might have a lead on some missing persons from the Beeker Star Ships Company."

He passed her his notebook.

"Avionics?"

"Simon might be a drone person."

Penelope looked impressed.

"Did anyone check with the government to see if Paul Beeker has contracts with them?"

"I've already given the information to the Captain. He will check with the people he knows at the Pentagon."

"The scientists sound interesting. Are we thinking any were drug makers?"

"We're checking their schooling and prior workplaces on all the names. With the information, we might better be able to speculate about some scenarios. Then again, the four people may show up to work tomorrow, and we start all over again."

Penelope mulled over the information.

"The warehouse owner, Roman Manning, was let go because of insufficient evidence. If these are the missing people, we might want to see if there is any connection to Mr. Manning."

"Very good. I haven't ruled the warehouse owner out just yet."

Penelope looked strange. Something was bothering her big time.

"There is something else wrong?"

8 Strange Email

Penelope didn't want to tell her boss. The relationship they shared was a delicate one. Personal overrode the professional. She was a big girl and a detective.

"Last week, I received a strange note and turned the note into the department that researches potential threats to officers."

Liam couldn't believe his wife. Timing and trust were everything.

"Last week you received this threatening note, and you tell me now? You are my employee."

She nodded. Liam looked at the ceiling.

"Today, I received a second note. This note contains the same words as the first. The department thinks the person is pulling pranks."

"Who has the notes?"

"Tim Brewster."

Liam didn't like Tim. They never hit things off when introduced.

"You know the notes would go to Jonathan who would turn them over to me."

Penelope didn't answer him.

"I sent you a copy of the notes a few minutes ago."

Liam pulled the notes up on his computer, read them, and stored them in a file.

"This is a standard, every day, textbook harassment note."

She got up to leave.

"You receive another one, and what are you going to do, detective?"

She paused.

"Yes, sir."

Liam watched his wife, "And?"

Penelope left his office quietly. She didn't answer him. Liam expected an apology. He remembered their first day together. She didn't obey him when he told her to stay in the car. Penelope didn't obey him then, and she wasn't going to start now.

"Women!"

Hugh stepped over his threshold and turned around to quickly exit.

"No, you don't. Come back here."

Hugh looked frazzled.

"I can come back when you are in a better mood."

"Who says I'm not in a good mood?"

Hugh left the door open.

"There's not much information because the police department is having a picnic today. Their database is having ups and downs. I did contact the Immigration people, and only three have temporary work visas. All three persons' visas were set to expire in three months. They didn't submit for an extension that we know about. Mrs. Beeker might have more information. The fourth person, Simon, is a citizen."

Liam watched Hugh.

"You knew about the harassment notes my wife received?"

Hugh looked guilty. He opened his mouth to talk and closed it again. Penelope asked him to remain quiet.

"Next time, you will tell me, Hugh. She's my detective and my wife. Let me park the heavy emphasis on the wife."

"Yes, sir."

Hugh backed out of Liam's office. He mumbled to himself and ran into Carter.

"Carter quit following me around."

Carter looked at Liam for support. Liam got up and slammed his door. The last person he wanted to talk with right now was Carter or anyone in the building.

Hugh always was a good friend to Penelope. He wasn't at all surprised she talked to him first. He heard Carter swear. Liam looked out his window to see Carter with a broken desk drawer in his hands.

Liam touched his beautiful wood desk. The drawers worked and were lockable. He took the keys out of his pocket and locked his office door.

He stood by Penelope's desk.

"How about dinner near or on the wharf?"

Penelope finished watering her large fern plants.

"Are you buying?"

Liam took her arm.

"I always do."

Penelope glanced over her shoulder at Carter.

"You should tell him that you switched the drawer."

"Not on your life. He needs to learn how to use an electric screwdriver."

Hugh walked with them to their vehicles.

"I bought a tent today at lunch. The rods were difficult. There are casting ones, trolling gear, big, or little lures, and line weight plus bobbers and plastic worms. Who uses plastic worms?"

"Everybody does who owns a rod and reel."

"The worms look like my kid's candy. We could try the sour ones."

Liam gave him the thumbs-up sign. Penelope looked at Liam questioningly.

"We're going camping and fishing with Dodge some weekend. Dodge is checking for clean natural lakes."

Penelope wasn't even going to ask what prompted the invitation. They climbed into the black sports car. Liam drove easily on the freeway.

"Three big juveniles scaring little fish with the wrong rod, line, and lures. The large fish are laughing at the sour candy."

Liam knew she was fine. He was getting there.

"Don't worry. Dodge is going to help him get the proper gear. I'm responsible for food and fire."

Penelope believed Liam was good with both. She wondered about the fishing trip. Dodge never drove past a fishing store without stopping. The man probably owned a hundred lures by now.

"Should I buy the chef's aprons?"

"Nah, we'll use our t-shirts."

"Is that why men have holes in their shirts?"

"You saw my shirts in the garage."

Penelope waited until he parked the car.

"Ready?"

She gave him her hand after he opened the car door. The couple mingled with the rest of the tourists on the pier. The smells of fried fish hit their senses. Going to any of the restaurants in the area was interesting. The chefs' culinary skills were top-notch. Even the vegetables tasted different. She could smell the garlic and unusual spices.

"I'm starving."

9 Surveillance Plan

Liam read the file on the four dead people. After two more weeks, the police had positively identified the four employees of the Beeker's company. Paul Beeker paid for the employees' funerals, and as temporary workers the families received compensation. The amount was nothing compared to what the employees could have made during their lifetime.

He put the file down and watched his Captain.

"There is no evidence to connect their deaths to Paul Beeker, nor do we have any idea who set the fire or created the drug lab. There were no prints found in his refrigeration unit which he voluntarily allowed the Mexican police to examine."

Liam rubbed his finger over his stubble. He didn't have time to shave this morning. He always shaved. The time was six o'clock. His boss was leaving to go out of town for a week's vacation.

"Try to find something while I'm gone."

Liam understood.

"Have a good time with your family."

Jonathan shook hands with his lead detective.

"Whatever you decide, I'll go along. You know the routine. Shut the door when you leave. I've hit the lock."

His boss left him alone to think. Liam looked at the awards in the Captain's office. There were many of them in a glass case. He and Jonathan worked together for a long time. The way they approached a case was similar. Dodge was a part of that group. Hugh came aboard a little later.

"Who broke the container lock? Were the four people inside of a refrigerator container? They wouldn't enter voluntarily. Someone held a gun and forced them inside some type of refrigeration unit. Where was the benefit of killing them? Why didn't the times of their deaths match? Were they part of the drug lab at the warehouse? What else was happening in the lab? How did the bodies get there?"

Liam knew simple was never part of a murder. Some person or persons planned the final chapter.

"Perhaps there was no choice. The murderer needed to kill them. Did someone see something they shouldn't have? What other illegal shipments could have existed? Does Paul know something? What about his wife? How do you kill and get away?"

Liam went out of Jonathan's door and let the door swing shut. He tried the knob. The boss's office was secure. He went into his office. At seven o'clock, Penelope joined him.

"Hey, stranger."

Liam poured her a cup of coffee.

"Hey, yourself. You slept an extra hour."

She took the hot cup guiltily.

"I thought I would come in early and help you think."

She noticed her husband hadn't shaved. He also wasn't sleeping well after the interview with Paul.

"We should start spying on people. Perhaps there is a shipment that got canceled due to errors. Dead bodies might be the error. Confusion happens. The person will try to correct the situation. They won't run away so easily after all this effort has been expended. Setting up an illegal operation takes time."

Liam tapped his fingers on his desk. The door to the investigation just opened a little wider. He understood chaos or confusion. Something unplanned might have happened.

"Thank you, detective."

"You are welcome."

She watched as Liam started scribbling a plan on paper. Penelope waited. After half an hour, Hugh arrived with fresh-baked bakery scones. He took one and handed the bag to Penelope. She smelled the aroma and selected a scone with golden raisins and white frosting. She put the bag on Liam's desk. Automatically, he took one out and set the cinnamon scone on a napkin. Cinnamon anything was his favorite. Hugh did well this morning remembering everyone's favorite. He winked.

Liam bit into the scone. He took a second and third bite.

"We begin by monitoring the warehouses. The warehouse is where the action started. I'll get Dodge to get hired as a security guard with his dog at a warehouse next to the one that burned. There was an ad in the newspaper. They advertised the position with an immediate start date. Davidson can use special cameras to watch the trucks coming and going with Dodge. When the Star Caroline II docks, we'll ask the police to monitor the ship. I'll see when the tanker is scheduled to return. Hugh and Carter will follow Paul Beeker. He doesn't know either man. Penelope and I will follow

Jane Beeker. We'll take lots of pictures. I want to see license plates, so we can track their visitors. Dates and times must be written down. At the end of each day, people report to me verbally, via text, or email."

Hugh rubbed his hands together.

"A good old-fashioned surveillance plan is perfect. I like your type of thinking. I'll bring my nighttime binoculars and a bulletproof vest. I've got this cool flashlight that blinds bats. My kids bought me a cheerleader's mega horn for Christmas. My new camouflage jeans and shirt the wife gave me for my birthday with combat boots finish my outfit. I knew this day would come. However, you should put Carter with Dodge."

Liam finished his scone. He shook his head in the negative.

"Oh, come on, Liam. I thought we were friends. I called ahead. The bakery made the bigger scones today."

Liam appreciated the scones so much he took a second cinnamon one out of the bag. Hugh was encouraged.

"Dodge can't stand Carter. You know how he gets around detectives not paying attention. Carter would be on the floor in less than five minutes. The scones are appreciated."

Hugh rolled his eyes.

"How about the new female detective?"

"She's too green to understand Dodge."

Hugh sighed and decided on one more tactic.

"The guy crunches on carrots. Next, he eats cucumbers, and lastly, it's the celery in a homemade dip which he spills every time on his expensive slacks. Then there are the shoes. Nobody wears black dress shoes to work. Carter can't get out of the car because he looks like a cop. The man is a nut case and drives me crazy."

"At least Dodge will be sane."

Penelope touched Hugh's arm.

"We might be able to switch off. I think the newbie Detective Susan Clemens might work well with Carter. He's been training her. I read her file. She shoots a gun super well. The center target was filled at the gun range when I ran into her last week. Plus, we, as a team, might need Hugh as an alternate fill-in person."

"Great idea. See, Penelope likes me. I didn't know Susan was that good at shooting. Dodge might like her."

Liam acknowledged they couldn't be on surveillance all the time.

"Hugh, you coordinate with Davidson and Carter. Carter can coordinate with Susan. You get days, and they can do the later hours. Now that we have the surveillance planned, are there any other questions?"

His wife raised her hand.

"I'd like more than one gun."

"Me, too," said Hugh.

"All right. I'll get everyone extra guns. Hugh, you can sign them out. Any more questions?"

Hugh raised his hand. Liam knew the question.

"Yes, you can deduct your lunch. Go buy yourself a large ham and loaves of bread."

"What about potato salad?"

He looked at Hugh.

"Emma knows how to make the salad, so it will be cheaper and will freeze."

"Potato salad is included. Are we done? Penelope and I need to talk about a vehicle. I think we should use company cars and rentals. In other words, no car is used twice by any of the teams."

"Offsite coffee?"

Liam groaned.

"Yes, I'll buy coffee. Send me the tab."

Hugh nodded.

"I'm off. I'll let the others know the game plan."

"Hugh, I'll talk with Dodge."

The detective left the office. The room was quiet without Hugh's booming voice. There were many questions they would need to uncover. The beginning of an investigation was rather boring. She preferred the middle part when they held more facts in their deck.

Facts gave a case its momentum. One fact built upon the other like a stack of cards. The trick was walking through the tower of cards without knocking one over. Good balance was required and a steady step.

"What happens when we find something?"

Liam knew stakeouts or surveillances were risky.

"We cover each other and report. No one takes unnecessary risks unless there is no other option."

He noticed her drawing a tower of poker playing cards. He saw the king, queen, and joker card repeated in her stack.

"Nice drawing. You used black cards and not the red ones. Any special reason for the black?"

"Red means danger. I think this game will be filled with the stuff. I was trying for an avoidance picture."

"Did the avoidance picture work?"

"No. I believe this case will be extremely messy."

Liam watched his wife. Sometimes her intuitive nature scared him. Penelope was her own woman and didn't fold or bend easily. He reasoned that was the attraction. *She stood her ground.*

She scribbled over her drawing and wrote down on a piece of paper the gun she wanted. She shoved the paper toward him.

"Getting back to the present, I think the firepower of the enemy is about the same caliber."

Liam knew Penelope was more than likely correct.

"We'll get one for each team. Happy, now?"

"Immensely. Tell me the scoop on Jane Beeker."

Liam told her the information that he knew.

"You said she has a sister. Does the sister work for the Beeker Company?"

"She isn't listed as an employee. There is an apartment address for her."

He gave her the address.

"I think she might be here as a student."

"Do you want me to check her out?"

Liam didn't want to waste time. The detectives would have enough on their plates.

"We can pass for now. Let's see who Mrs. Beeker has for visitors each day. I'd like to see what she does with her time, and who her friends are?"

Penelope understood. She did think one thing was odd.

"You didn't want to do the stakeout on Paul. Is there any special reason?"

Liam couldn't explain. He gave it a try.

"There was a look in his eyes when he realized you were my wife. I think there might be something there. That's why we are monitoring the wife."

"Emptiness. I saw a brief flicker."

Liam knew Penelope put a name to what he saw.

"I could be wrong."

She didn't think her husband missed much either.

"When do you want a rental car?"

"Let's pick up one after work. I'm thinking a large car would work that fits the neighborhood. I do have some chicken kebobs in the freezer we can eat tonight. I'm thinking we can get some food for sandwiches and start our part tomorrow night. We work from six to one in the morning to see if anything is happening. Next, we come home and sleep for six hours and do the day shift. Days will be important to establish her base routine. Weekends, we'll do nights."

"I'll make a list for the grocery store."

His wife disappeared, and Liam started making his calls. He arranged for rental cars.

10 Week One on Surveillance

The reports were on Liam's computer. He arranged a conference call with his surveillance teams.

"Thank you, everyone, for your dedication this week. We are on a secure network. The department is trying a different company. Make sure you hide your passwords. I'll try to summarize what we have found so far."

Penelope and Hugh were in Liam's office with Jonathan.

"Dodge and Davidson's report on the warehouse shows some interesting developments. Ten new and small capacity delivery trucks were brought onto the warehouse next to the one that burned. They are parked on the lot near the large warehouse doors. Dodge believes the trucks are currently empty because nothing was unloaded. At the time of the truck delivery, the owner of the warehouse Roman Manning arrived. He talked with the warehouse foreman, and they met the Beeker lawyer, Rauf Merk. All three went inside the warehouse. We aren't sure why Mr. Merk was at this meeting unless he also is Mr. Manning's lawyer. The relatives of the victims may be suing the burned warehouse for negligence."

Liam turned over some papers and found what he was looking for on the next page and read the document.

"Our Captain has confirmed five of the victim's relatives are suing Manning for the wrongful death of their loved ones as of today. We have the court date for the guard Mr. Hector."

Hugh asked a question.

"Where did Mr. Manning buy the trucks? I thought he was running low on money what with a burned warehouse, an expensive lawyer, and now a pending lawsuit."

"Good question. Dodge is checking around with the truck dealerships. At this point, we have no connection to Beeker other than they use the same lawyer."

Dodge joined the meeting a few minutes earlier via his phone. He interjected.

"The trucks were purchased by a man named Benny Lourdes."

Liam looked at his boss.

"Benny Lourdes was incarcerated for five years for illegal shipping of salvage cars to Mexico without proper authorization. I'll check, but it appears he may be out of prison. Good research on the trucks. Lourdes might have found another illegal investment opportunity. If he is interested in Manning, we might have new developments at the warehouse complex."

Penelope wrinkled her brow.

"The delivery trucks are small. I wonder why? Aren't car parts large?"

Liam interjected.

"The shipment might be smaller parts. We're thinking the four professionals that were killed might have been working on a new design of a product in high demand for the underground network."

Hugh read the file on the four dead people.

"We might be looking for small drones."

"Illegal, highly sophisticated military-grade drones to be exact. If someone can produce them and keep a supply chain going, we're talking big money," mentioned Liam.

The lead detective waited for the teams to calm down.

"Carter and Susan's report on Paul Beeker showed nothing promising. His wife returned from her spa vacation. They ate dinner out twice, and he worked at his office. He met with his lawyer once and with some shipping captains at his place of work. Then he played golf for two days at their country club. He had drinks with people from work at the club. He visited the apartment of Jane's sister once to talk with the maid about cleaning the apartment. The sister didn't seem to be home."

A few of the other detectives asked questions.

"I've created a file of the report summary and the pictures everyone took. If there are any corrections to my summary, let me know. Please review the pictures. They might be critical to solving this case. Now for Penelope and my report on Jane Beeker. We did track her one evening and saw her go out to dinner with her husband and later go swimming in her pool."

Penelope remembered the couple in the water. They kept their distance from each other.

"Mrs. Beeker has a routine beauty and dermatologist appointment each week at the same time. She went to work like normal but went home in the afternoons. We found it interesting that she met with her lawyer, Rauf Merk three times. They ate lunch outside near the pool. We wished there were microphones on the patio. The conversation between the two might have been interesting. She hugged him goodbye after each meeting. An Immigration official also visited the house. We are trying to find out why the officer was there. She also met the senior ship officer, Juan Hermosa, outside near the pool. They were in a heated argument and stopped when Paul Beeker unexpectedly came home. Mr. Hermosa left. Paul looked angry and went back into the house."

Hugh spoke.

"This sounds like trouble in paradise. I wonder what is wrong?"

"I could wiretap the house," said Dodge.

Jonathan refrained from smiling.

"Unfortunately, the judge won't approve one yet."

"There are other listening devices we can use. Any houses in the area for rent within range?"

"Good question, Dodge. I'll contact a real estate agent and find out," said Penelope.

Liam was pleased with his team.

"The ship, Star Caroline II, returns in a month. Let's stop the surveillance of the people except for Dodge and Davidson. Dodge will remain a security guard at the warehouse. Davidson will visit him as his friend to relieve the dog. We have some additional research to do on Manning, Lourdes, and Hermosa. Hugh will take Manning and Lourdes. Susan and Carter will take Hermosa. Penelope and I will take Merk, Paul, and Jane. If there are no questions, have a good weekend everyone."

The line disconnected. Jonathan congratulated Liam on his surveillance plan and mentioned that he would ask around his friends about the Merk and Beeker's relationship. He left Liam's office.

Hugh topped off his coffee and grabbed a chair.

"This drone business could be interesting or bad."

"We know," said Liam.

"I've done some reading about unmanned systems and the FAA. My good neighbor across the street has a drone and works for the FAA. His cats sneak out of the house, and he uses the drone to find them. The drone lands with the cat treats in a little pouch. The cat opens the pouch and eats. He catches the cat. We might want to set up a meeting and talk with him."

"Excellent. I'm interested in how we might interrupt a drone's flight, and what gear can be put on a drone."

Hugh drank his coffee.

"The model he showed me was something they caught on a guy flying the drone across the border between California and Arizona. The drone was small and could fire some bullets."

Penelope read about an upcoming event in San Diego.

"There's a show in San Diego put on by various manufacturers who make drones. We might want to attend. It's on the next weekend after this one. Dodge might also attempt visiting the show without you boys."

"I'll let Dodge know."

11 Surfing and Strange Object

Liam and Penelope drove to their condominium for the weekend. While they were on surveillance, they stayed at Liam's house close to the beach in Los Angeles.

"I'm glad we are spending time at our condominium this weekend. I love our three-bedroom condo unit. The groceries we brought should last us for the weekend."

Liam put his and her suitcase down. He held his wife.

"We can eat out and freeze the groceries. I'd like this weekend to be calm. When are your parents arriving at their condominium unit?"

"My dad said they would get here tomorrow and will be staying for two weeks."

"Wendy and Warren King. It will be nice to see them. They will want to go out to eat. They know you don't cook."

"My parents like your steaks and handmade French fries."

"They do, don't they?"

"Yes."

Liam helped his wife put away the groceries.

"I'm going to talk with the security guard to see what has been happening while we were gone."

"I'll check out the beach and be back in five to ten minutes."

Penelope watched as Liam left. She put her shorts and sandals on and went down to the beach.

There was little wind this evening, and the air was still warm. There was some light on the horizon. She didn't go down to the water's edge but stood closer to the condominium building.

She turned because of a humming sound. There was a black object flying toward her. Penelope ran toward the table area and ducked under a metal table. The drone flew above the table and then away. She crawled out from under the table and ran upstairs.

Liam joined her. As soon as he saw her face, he knew something was wrong.

"The beach was scary. I didn't go to the water's edge. I was glad because someone flew a tiny drone. The drone came after me. There was a barrel gadget."

Liam grabbed his gun and cell phone. He raced to the beach. Penelope did the same and ran after him. They stood on the beach sand.

"Show me where you were standing and in what direction the drone came."

She stood and pointed.

"Come on."

They hiked down the beach for a mile. They didn't see anyone.

"Most drones have a three-mile limit. Some larger ones can do five miles. I believe the person with the drone has left the vicinity. I will report the drone to the police and Hugh's neighbor."

They walked back to the condominium, and she showed him where she hid. Upon reaching their unit, Liam called the police. He also contacted Hugh, Dodge, and Carter to warn them.

"We can't go surfing tomorrow."

Penelope looked disappointed.

"There have been some shark sightings. From what the security guard saw, the sharks were smaller and maybe coming in for the abundance of minnows that seem to have traveled northward. I vote we stay out of the water this weekend."

"I'm all right with no surfing. We can use the indoor pool."

Liam started making hamburger patties. Penelope buttered the buns and cleaned the lettuce. After they assembled the cooked hamburgers, Liam grabbed them colas.

"I'm glad the drone didn't hurt you. I was worried when you told me about this drone. I wonder if the drone was meant to scare us off from our investigation. Maybe we have gotten too close to someone."

Penelope thought about the drone.

"Normally, drones fly high. This one was flying low. The person must have been close enough to see me on the drone camera. The drone sound was almost a hum."

"We're talking expensive and high tech."

"Should I be worried about my parents staying here?"

Liam believed the drone wouldn't return for a while. The police would be patrolling the area.

"Your parents should be fine. We'll tell them about the drone and the sharks."

"There goes our calm weekend."

Liam took their plates and put them in the dishwasher. He filled the hamburger pan with soap and water and washed it. Rinsing the pan, he laid it on a towel on the counter.

"Now we can be calm and get a little snuggling in while we watch the news."

They watched a tanker in the water which was on fire near the Los Angeles Harbor. Dredges were spraying water on the large ship. The news helicopter came close to the ship, and they saw a star emblem. Liam undid his arm around Penelope and went into the other room to contact his boss.

She backed up the program and hit the record button. Her husband would want to see the video in its entirety. She wondered if this was a hit on Paul Beeker by an enemy or an accident. She remembered the painting in the library of the broken ship on the beach. There would be an investigation into the fire. She hoped the ship didn't sink.

Liam returned from his call in their den.

"The ship is the Star Magnetic and belongs to Paul. One of the compartments caught fire and tried to engulf two others. The hoses were successful in stopping further damage. The fire looked suspicious. We'll know tomorrow."

"I was thinking about the drone show. You should go with my father. Hugh could take his son and Dodge might go with a date. Susan can accompany Carter. Davidson will monitor the warehouse. That way, things will look normal and not like a bunch of nervous detectives descending on the drone manufacturers."

"You are right. Each of us should focus on an aspect of the drone. I'm thinking materials, infrared cameras, GPS and non-satellite, remote ground control and propulsion systems, sensors in the nose, obstacle detection, thermal vision, etc."

She hugged her husband. He rubbed her hair.

"I think we should call this day over."

"Aye, aye, captain."

"Next week, your father might like to visit a military base and see some Predator and Reaper drones."

"He would enjoy the day very much. I think while the boys are playing, my mom and I will do some shopping. You and I saw Jane Beeker go into very exclusive clothing, makeup, and jewelry stores. We might run into her."

"Did I tell you lately how sneaky you have become?"

"This means I can spend all I want in the stores."

Liam stuttered and she punched his arm.

"I'll try to restrain myself."

Her husband rubbed his arm as if he were in pain. She ignored him.

"I wonder if Emma would like to go with us next Saturday."

Liam shook his head.

"Hugh might think otherwise."

"We'll say Saturday is a ladies' long lunch day."

"More of the sneaky."

Liam jumped out of her way and grabbed her arm. He kissed his wife.

"Now who's sneaky."

12 Drone Show

Hugh and his son were watching a drone demonstration when Liam and Warren King approached.

"Hi, Warren, glad to see you and your wife arrived safely in Los Angeles. I hope someone is watching the cows in Billings."

Warren grinned and pumped Hugh's hand. Hugh's son stuck out his hand, and Warren was gentler with the handshake.

Warren signaled the manufacturer's rep and talked with him. After five minutes, the demonstrator let Warren handle the drone. Warren did flips with the drone and returned the device.

"Nice going. Where did you learn to fly drones?" asked Liam.

"We purchased some last year to keep track of our herds of cattle. The drones are extremely effective until you run into tall trees. Fortunately, we don't have that many on our ranch. We like the larger, long-distance drones. They can fly about five miles. It took a while for the horses to get used to the noise."

Hugh's son pointed to the food area.

"We're going to grab a bite to eat."

Warren and Liam watched them disappear through a doorway. Dodge came through the same doorway a minute later.

"You missed Hugh and his son."

"Hello, Liam. Warren, good to see you."

Warren saw the young woman standing next to the retired detective.

"Who's your date?"

"This is Detective Susan Clemens. Carter couldn't make the show."

Liam wasn't surprised. Susan saw Liam's displeasure.

"Carter not being here is my fault. I shut the car door on his hand while he was wiping the mayo dip off his slacks last night."

Dodge smiled at Liam.

"We came early to the show and were the first ones in line. I've had a good time talking with the manufacturers, but I need to get back to work. My boss is a terrible taskmaster."

Warren grinned.

"We'll put some steaks on the grill when you aren't working so hard."

"I look forward to eating with you and Wendy. Come on Susan. Let's get out of here before the crowd blocks our exit."

Liam and Warren walked around the various displays. Warren was interested in a manufacturer. He stopped to talk. Liam saw Paul Beeker go into the small drones' room.

"Excuse me, Paul Beeker is here. The department is working on a new case, and I need to talk with him for a minute."

"No problem. If I'm not with the manufacturer, I'll be in the food court."

Liam went into the small drone room. He watched Paul for ten minutes talking to one manufacturer. Liam strolled over to the booth and picked up a small drone. The drones were tethered to cords so people couldn't steal them. An assistant asked if he needed help.

"Tell me why I should purchase your drone versus the booth next to you. Both booths appear popular."

"Our drone is the smallest and quietest on the market. The propulsion system is superb, and our ability to accurately measure the distance to objects makes them the perfect drone. Also, our warranty and replacement of parts are better."

The demo man showed him how the parts folded to disappear.

"They also fly higher and further using a radio signal. The more expensive drones are to your right."

Liam noticed the expensive price tag on the one he held in his hands.

"How much more expensive are the ones on the right side?"

"Thousands more, sir."

Liam blew out a whistle. Paul turned. He put the pricey drone down and walked over.

"Imagine my surprise in seeing you at this show. I didn't know you were into drone technology, especially in this price range."

Liam looked Paul in the eye.

"My father-in-law is visiting. We thought we would come to the show while the women went shopping. He has some larger drones he uses in Montana on his ranch to keep track of his cows. I thought I would look at the smaller drones. This booth seemed the crowd favorite."

"Cow tracking is a new idea. I have read about ranchers using the drone. They like this one manufacturer which is in the other room."

Liam mentioned the name.

"Yes, that is the correct one."

Warren stepped beside his daughter's husband.

"All they make in the food court were hotdogs, pizza, and French fries. I think we should eat at a restaurant. No fish though. We've eaten fish twice already. I like lake fish better."

"Paul Beeker, this is my father-in-law, Warren King."

Warren and Paul shook hands.

"I hear you have large ships and carry grain to Mexico."

"And you, Mr. King own an extremely large ranch with cows per my friend. You like drones."

Warren carried several drone brochures in his two jacket pockets with the manufacturer rep's business card attached.

"Yes, we do. The drones work well in Montana. Sometimes we lose them in the snowdrifts. A few of ours contained bad compasses. We used the horses to find the downed drones. We also grow our grain in the summer. We have the large machines come in for the cutting. Usually, the grain is sold to farmers in our state."

"Good to see you again, Paul. I need to get my father-in-law some food before we return. I know a great place near the ocean that does beef."

Paul nodded.

"Hayden's, enjoy the burritos."

After they were outside, Warren spoke.

"The man isn't your friend."

Liam opened his sports car door.

"The man is way out of my league."

"Penelope told me that Paul Beeker owns the Star Ships Company. You are talking a lot of coins. I didn't like his old man very much. He was too intense."

13 Liam and Warren

Liam drove his black sports car to his favorite restaurant on a beach. The two men walked through the sand to reach the food shack.

"Hi, Hayden, we'd like two of your beef burritos with the sauce on the side with the beans. Make the meat-heavy and we'd like the mild sauce. Two each and one cola each with limes."

The men took their burritos and drinks. They sat down at a whitewashed picnic table with an umbrella. There was a breeze off the ocean which kept the bugs away. After twenty minutes of eating, Warren commented.

"Those two burritos were the best I've tasted. Hayden knows how to season and cook a good roast to the ultimate tenderness."

"His father helps him smoke the meat, and there's final cooking in the oven. The final cook is slow with a diluted sauce mixture they've used for years. He told me there's vinegar, brown sugar, and unique spices. In other words, they like to buy spices from all over. I imagine the spices aren't cheap. He sells out by two or two-thirty every day in the summer."

"Next time, I'll try the medium sauce. I might live in Montana, but I like a little more heat."

Liam watched the people mingling on the beach.

"Thank you for taking me to see the large government drones and the drones at the show. Buying me lunch made my day. This was fun."

"You are welcome. Your daughter suggested the drone show."

"Tell me about this case. Penelope said you were working strange hours."

Liam shook his head. His wife warned him that her father would ask.

"We're working a case that's going nowhere. Six people died. Four of those people were professionals in the wrong job or the wrong place."

"You think this Beeker fella has something to do with their deaths?"

"We aren't exactly sure. His father was strict and ran his business to the letter of the law."

Warren understood.

"Times change. There's more pressure these days. Everyone wants a piece of the prize. Tanker ships don't come cheap. We're talking millions to dump one in the water. Then there's dock fees, red tape, paperwork, and fuel costs. More people are cutting corners to keep up. Things disappear and are never reported. Maybe Beeker shoves things under the table on occasion. I wouldn't blame him. The police have a harder job."

"I will agree. The cases have become more complicated to solve. At least, I have a good team. Your daughter is a big help."

"Good to know. She always was a hard worker. Paul seemed friendly enough. He looked a little bit flustered to see you. I watched from the doorway for a couple of minutes."

"He was caught off guard."

"Well, good luck with this one. I wonder if either one of us has any money left in our checking accounts."

Liam knew his father-in-law was ready to go back.

"I was too afraid to look."

He drove while Warren took a nap on their way to Los Angeles. Liam stopped at the headquarters building so Warren could see his new office. They ran into Jonathan, and the two men chatted.

Liam contacted his wife.

"Don't worry. We bought some cooked chicken, coleslaw, buns, and beans for supper on our way to the condo."

"Great. The show was excellent, and I ran into Paul Beeker. He was looking at expensive, high tech small drones. I'll tell you about the drones later."

"Mom and I bought some nice slack outfits for the evening and some for the beach. Also, we purchased sandals and beach bags. No jewelry. The cheapest was about five grand."

"Your dad is coming out of Jonathan's office. We should be there in thirty-five to forty-five minutes."

Jonathan approached Warren as Liam locked his office door.

"I did find something about Rauf Merk."

Liam paused curiously to hear.

"Merk worked at the law firm that represented Benny Lourdes during his trial on the salvage cars."

"Interesting connection between the two men. I ran into Paul Beeker at the drone show."

Jonathan looked at his watch.

"The police commissioner called me. I asked him to check on any drones flying around your condominium. No registered drones with the FAA were flying in the area."

"Too bad I didn't see the drone to take a shot. We could have studied the parts to find the manufacturer."

Jonathan shook his head. Liam was in total agreement. "The manufacturer might not be listed either."

Jonathan turned to Warren.

"Come visit us anytime."

Warren and Liam watched the Captain walk away.

"Someone would need to draw the parts, make molds, and have an entire operation to assemble the drones, not to mention install the software."

"I know. A needle in a haystack is what we are trying to find."

"The needle or the parts might be made in another country," offered Warren.

Liam thought about his father-in-law's comment.

"The girls bought us chicken for supper."

"What are we waiting for Liam? We have beautiful women at home with hot food. Those two combinations are all I need to survive."

"Women and food."

"Yes, sir. Sometimes hot and sometimes cold. I don't mind."

Liam wondered about the comment.

"You'll find out soon enough. We were glad she transferred to Los Angeles instead of San Diego."

"Penelope was looking at San Diego for a job. I never knew."

"She changed her mind. There were too many single men on the force. Penelope believed Los Angeles's force was a safer bet. Then she ran into you."

Liam stopped.

"We're delighted. Things have a way of working out."

Warren went out the exit door, and Liam trailed behind. The old man could move when he wanted. He was right behind him.

When they returned to the condominium, Liam kissed his wife.

"You were going to San Diego?"

Penelope sent an evil eye to her father.

"Dad?"

Warren and Wendy went outside on the patio.

"There was some discussion. Here, you set the table. I'm exhausted from shopping."

14 Party Invitation

The Star Magnetic ship fire was started by some disgruntled workers who were fighting. They quickly were arrested and placed in jail. Paul Beeker's company insurance would pay for the damages. The tanker was towed into a shipyard for some hasty repairs before reinspection and release.

Wendy and Warren's two-week vacation ended, and they flew home to Montana.

Sunday evening Liam dropped Penelope off at his home and went to the restaurant to get their supper. On the way out of his beach house, he picked up the mail. While waiting for the takeout dinner, he perused the envelopes. One white envelope stood out with gold lettering. He quickly slit the envelope and read the invitation.

His order was ready. He paid the cashier and drove home. Sitting the containers on the bar countertop in the kitchen, Penelope joined him. She was in a soft robe and sat on the tall stool in her fuzzy slippers.

"This smells heavenly. Kung Pao, Sesame Chicken, and small bags of peanuts instead of fortune cookies. Heat and salty is always a good combination."

"The taste is awesome. Let's dig in while the chicken is warm."

After their stomachs were filled, he took the containers and combined the rest of the leftovers into two containers. Penelope picked up the mail and slowly went through the pile. There was one for trash and one for bills to pay. She halted at the opened invitation.

"What is in this white envelope?"

Liam washed his hands and took the kitchen towel. He turned around.

"I couldn't believe the card."

She opened the card and read the invitation.

"We are invited to a party Friday evening at Paul and Jane Beeker's mansion."

He placed the towel on the kitchen cupboard door.

"We should decline the invitation."

Penelope didn't agree.

"Please explain your reasoning to me."

"We are detectives investigating the man, his wife, and firm."

"Those gems are all the more reason we should go."

"No, we aren't going. The party is off the table. The risk is too high."

Penelope looked at her husband.

"Fine."

She left the kitchen and went upstairs.

Liam knew he should have thrown the invitation away. Now he was in trouble. His wife wanted to go. He didn't. There wasn't any way he was going to put Penelope that close to danger. He took the garbage out and went to their den to pay some bills.

When he was done, he crawled into bed. Penelope appeared fast asleep.

In the morning she was dressed and waiting for him when he came down to get coffee. He spoke to her, and she barely spoke back.

When they reached the office, she quickly exited the car. Liam sat in his sports car. Hugh parked next to him.

"Hi, Liam. Most people get out of their vehicles and go inside away from this heat."

"Shut up, Hugh."

Hugh rushed around to the passenger side and climbed in the car.

"First fights after the wedding are always the worst. Trust me, I know exactly how you feel. She's right and you're wrong."

"The Beeker's are having a party. Wrong is right. The invitation should have been destroyed. I told her we aren't going. She objected."

Hugh rubbed his hands together.

"I'll be your date for the evening."

Liam groaned.

"Hugh, just stuff it somewhere."

The elderly detective thought about the Beeker's. Right now, the family was an unknown and a potential hazard.

"Okay. I'm going away."

Hugh stepped out of the car and left the man alone.

Liam sat in the car for fifteen minutes trying to make a rational decision about the party. Finally, he went inside the building to his office. Penelope and Hugh were not around. After an hour, he went looking for his wife. He stopped at the desk of Jonathan's secretary.

"Have you seen Detective Knight?"

Jonathan's secretary looked up. "Missing a detective is never good. Jonathan saw her go to our conference room three on the floor below ours. He called me to let you know if you asked. Hugh's talking with Tim."

Liam hated that the entire office might know he lost a detective in the building.

"Don't worry, Liam. No one knows she hides out there on occasion. I only know because my reports get handed to another secretary who sits close to the conference room. Penelope used the room a lot when she first started. Sometimes she would come on the weekend. The secretaries were doing records retention, and we shared our potluck lunch with her a couple of times. She bought us lunch in return. Not even Kamilla or Hugh know about her escape pad."

"Good to know."

Jonathan's secretary watched Liam walk away. She called Jonathan.

"Penelope and Liam might be off-grid for some time."

Jonathan thanked his secretary.

15 Continuance about Invitation

He found Penelope in the conference room when he looked in the tiny window. Liam slammed his body against the wall. He rehearsed his speech. Finally, he entered and closed the door. He was glad he checked with Jonathan's secretary.

"Here you are. I've been to this conference room a hundred times. However, let me talk. Paul Beeker used to be known as the playboy of the century. I know he is married now, but the image still sticks in my brain. He has this keen ability to wrap women around his finger. The party will have tequila, and that makes for disaster."

Penelope stopped drawing circles.

"You have spies."

Liam wasn't about to reveal a valuable resource.

"How strong is the tequila?"

Liam was confused.

"What difference does the strength of tequila make? Usually, the good stuff is forty to forty-five percent. The percentage goes higher on the pricier bottles. The rich like the brand Beeker imports."

"I believe I can handle both bottles if that is what is worrying you."

Liam didn't know what to say. Penelope was still upset with him.

"How about we let someone higher like Jonathan decide? His opinion is valuable and unbiased."

Penelope picked up her pen and started doodling. Liam grabbed her hand.

"Okay, we go, and we are careful. No drinks unless we have charge water. I handle Paul."

"How do you know that Jane isn't more dangerous?"

Liam rubbed his chin which was smooth and clean-shaven.

"We should bring Dodge along, but that is a bad idea. He is watching a warehouse."

"What about Hugh? He looks harmless."

Liam thought about the party.

"No. We go alone. Hugh and Carter need to be close by in case we need to call in the calvary."

Liam waited. His wife looked at him.

"You need to stop trying to protect me. I'm a detective and can handle myself."

"I know. I forget sometimes. I'll run the plan through our boss for approval."

Penelope stood and walked out of the conference room. Liam shoved his chair against the wall. He rode the elevator alone and walked into Jonathan's office. He shut the door.

Hugh came over to Penelope's desk. He handed her a bag of scones.

"Peace offering. Cinnamon scone which is not the raisin kind. Your second choice was available."

"Thanks, Hugh."

He sat down.

"Any ground coffee left?"

She nodded.

Hugh made them a pot of coffee with his favorite blend.

"This is like old times. We've drunk bucket loads."

Penelope smiled.

"The Beeker's invited us to a party this Friday."

Hugh frowned. "Touchy subject."

Penelope turned her screen on and stopped.

"Yes."

Hugh sighed.

"I get Liam. I've grown used to the way the man thinks. Paul is this spoiled super-rich kid. Nobody liked those kids in school. Not that they went to our school, but they showed up at our favorite hangouts. They came to our clubs to escape the wasteland of no fun on their turf. Our bands were better. The music was off the charts. Our girls were prettier and hotter."

"We're not in high school."

Hugh felt Penelope missed the point.

"I was talking about college."

He looked through her plants.

"Your husband is still in the boss's office. Maybe the party is not a good idea. I would imagine the lack of security is a huge downer. People disappear and get hurt in this world. We don't know who is responsible."

Penelope bit her lip. "You think I pushed Liam too much?"

Hugh drank his coffee.

"Liam does a good job. There is a reason he is the lead in this office. He is smarter than the rest of the detectives. Most of the detectives agree and stay out of his way. You need to not interfere."

Penelope knew that Hugh was right.

"I overstepped boundaries."

Hugh nodded.

"Boundaries matter."

He left her. Penelope saw Liam walk out of the boss's office. She approached him cautiously.

"I have this restaurant in mind where we can eat sushi. The place is new, but the rating was excellent."

Liam went into his office and came back out. He handed her his car keys.

"Lead the way."

They sat and watched the man make their sushi order. Liam took a bite out of his shrimp and lobster roll. Penelope ate her vegetarian roll.

"I like the food and the chef. He knows how to make this taste like sushi."

"Hugh talked with me while you were in Jonathan's office. He made me realize something."

Liam grabbed another roll and popped it into his mouth.

"I need to apologize. You are the lead investigator, and I overstepped my bounds."

Liam grabbed a third sushi roll and kept eating. Penelope ate another roll.

He finished his meal and waited for her to finish. She handed him the last two rolls. He ate the vegetarian roll with soy sauce and wasabi.

"The Captain decided for us. We aren't going to the party. The timing could be detrimental is the reason."

Liam watched Penelope's eyes. They brimmed with tears. He put his arms around his wife.

"I am the lead, but there is someone higher than me. I presented your case but lost."

He paid for their lunch and they walked to the sports car. Liam drove and turned in the direction of his house.

"Where are we going?"

"The Captain told me that we needed to take a break. The stress was showing. He told me to go home and take you with me."

"Wise man," commented Penelope.

After closing the garage door, she waited in the living room on the couch. She was going to turn on the television. He took the remote and placed the device on the coffee table. Liam sat down next to her and held her hand.

"We'll get through this case. However, I'd like very much to be a good husband."

Penelope smiled.

"You are a good husband."

She laid her head on his shoulder.

He relaxed. Penelope grabbed a blanket, covered them, and closed her eyes. The two exhausted detectives fell asleep.

The sun drifted into the ocean. Around midnight they awoke and went upstairs to their bedroom. Liam helped her put on her new nightgown.

"Your mom helped find this fuzzy nightgown for me."

"Thank you. I know you hate fuzzy nighties."

They crawled in bed and slept until morning. Liam made scrambled eggs. They were late getting to the office. Jonathan nodded to Liam as he walked past his door.

16 Fishing Trip Discussion

Hugh sat in Liam's office on Tuesday and reread the file. Liam dropped his briefcase on his desk.

"Good morning, Hugh, the weather this week looks spectacular."

"I'm glad to see you are cheerful."

Liam smiled.

"I am most definitely a happy man. A little rest goes a long way. What is in your report?"

Hugh gave him Dodge and Davidson's report first.

"The ten white vans have disappeared during the night. Some men came and drove them away around two in the morning. They thought the late hour was unusual."

Hugh handed him Susan and Carter's report.

"Ten white vans are at the Beeker home transporting party supplies and white tents. The license plates match the vans that were at the warehouse."

Hugh handed him his report. Liam wasn't happy. The vans belonged to the Beeker's. Of course, they could use their vans. He continued reading aloud.

"Their lawyer has leased the warehouse we are watching. The Star Caroline II has been delayed two weeks in Mexico due to a shortage of inspectors from the flu. Good grief. With the party and the delay, it looks like any strange activity might be put on hold."

Hugh waited for Dodge's phone call. Liam answered.

"Dodge, I read about the white vans. You can be gone this weekend. Carter and Susan volunteered to relieve you and Davidson. That's great. We should leave this Thursday. You have a friend's airplane with floats. Have you ever been to this place? No. You are sure this is a good spot. Let me check with Penelope, and I'll get back to you."

Liam disappeared, and Hugh stirred in the creamer. He watched Liam talking with Penelope. Hugh started humming and looked at some fishing videos. There was a favorite where the man caught a Largemouth bass and struggled to bring the fish into a net. Liam returned.

"We should go on this fishing trip to northern Washington for the weekend. Dodge thinks we can fly out Thursday morning and return Sunday afternoon. He told me you went shopping last night for fishing rods and the rest of the gear. My wife is okay with the trip. This is exciting. How about Emma?"

Hugh laughed.

"Emma helped me pack last night. She told me I was getting crabby and used the scale wrong. You never see me get upset. I wanted to make sure I was under the weight limit Dodge gave me. She's making brownies this morning and freezing us some sandwiches."

Liam suddenly felt like the two men conspired together to put the weekend plan into motion.

"You do get cranky. I'm not going to blame the crabs. Remember to pack your guns. We might want to be extra cautious. Wild animals are not welcome, but they live in the woods. Rain gear would be good."

"Dodge warned me about the animals and the weather. We bought you a present. We'll match like the scout group kids."

Hugh handed a bag to Liam. Inside was a rain jacket, rain pants, rain hat, and fishing gloves.

"Gee, thanks, Hugh. This is nicer than my old rain gear and the correct sizes. You guessed correctly."

Hugh was glad his friend was in a good mood and wanted to go fishing.

"Penelope helped. We didn't buy the gloves that float. Dodge wanted the three-quarter length fingers instead. Dodge told me I could put a small chain on the hook on the gloves and wrap the chain around my fishing pole. Do you think I'll lose my pole in the water?"

"I've got the cheaper gloves that float, but these are more practical. I do like them. About your question, you might want to try the chain."

Hugh left Liam's office as he tried on the gloves. Liam sent a note to his boss regarding vacation. He flexed his hand and pretended to cast with a fake rod in the gloves. The approval note came back in five minutes.

"Send me pictures of the one that got away," texted Jonathan.

Liam would send him a picture of the empty hook lying in the water in the sand next to a large rock. He left to buy groceries for the trip. He grabbed a few lightweight coolers and collapsible water jugs.

When his wife reached home, the gear was all over the living room and kitchen. She stepped through the minefield on the floor.

"I thought you were going to be gone three nights."

Liam looked at his clothes.

"There's too much. I could use some help."

Penelope grabbed a few necessary items.

"These are important."

Liam watched as she adeptly decided all the important items. They fit inside his large knapsack.

"You're a good packer. How about the food and drinks?"

She helped in the repackage of some food items. They put them on a separate shelf. She put red stickers on the freezer packages, so her husband could grab them in the morning.

"Did you buy ice?"

Liam smacked his forehead.

His wife turned up the ice maker. She found the heavier plastic bags and filled one of them. She put a red sticker on the ice.

"We can fill the second bag in the morning with the water jugs."

Liam put stickers on the plastic bag, water jugs, and coolers.

"My fishing gear is in the car. I shouldn't put red stickers on them."

Penelope agreed.

17 Fishing and Camping

Thursday morning, the three detectives flew to a secluded natural lake in Washington state. The men unloaded their gear and set up camp. Dodge and Liam were in one tent, and Hugh was in his tent with the food and fishing gear.

The men started a fire and cooked some steaks. After eating the filet mignons and salad, they decided to check the depth of the lake on the map to determine where the fish might hang out. Dodge saw the weed beds as they flew over the lake. Largemouth bass hid in the weeds. He pointed to the deeper water where they might find larger fish.

They heard another group of campers across the lake and watched as a blowup dinghy with a small motor attached hit their shore. Two men stepped out onto the tiny beach.

The strangers talked about fishing and wildlife. The campers were leaving in the morning, and the detectives would be alone on the lake. They disappeared in their dinghy.

"The stranger mentioned that we might want to move our camp across the lake," said Dodge.

Liam looked at the two tents, the floatplane, and their firepit.

"We would have to undo everything. It is late. I think we should stay."

"Liam, I am a little tired and this spot looks sweet. We stay. Let's not tell Hugh about the bear sighting."

Hugh came out of his tent. He whipped out some firecrackers, bottle rockets, and large sparklers. He thought they would be useful and fun. Now that they would be alone on the lake, they could create a racket.

He gave each person their fair share of the fireworks and a lighter device.

Dodge clicked on the lighter.

"Nice flame. We probably shouldn't light these inside the tent."

Liam lit his lighter.

"I don't know. We didn't bring candles."

Hugh sputtered.

"Come on. Put those lighters out. I didn't bring any extra fuel. But I do like to be prepared for a show. Some of the rockets go boom."

Dodge asked, "Which ones go boom?"

He showed him the box.

"See this box is bright red all around. Red is for loud and hot."

"Hot? Why did you say hot?"

Hugh laughed.

"Extra glow-factor and heat my friend. Make sure you run after you light one. Anyway, let's have some of those brownies Emma made."

The men turned in for the evening.

Friday morning, they motored the floatplane to the spot they selected. The men had fun catching large bass and a trout off the airplane floats and their blowup dinghy. After fishing, they motored the airplane to the shore next to their campsite and again secured the airplane.

Dodge cleaned the fish, and they started their fire. The fish was fried. They ate fish and chips for their dinner. The sandwiches disappeared during lunch. Hugh dug out the peanut butter cookies.

The men talked about women and went to bed. On Saturday, they returned to the same spot and caught two more trout. In the evening they cooked the fish. The canned beans with molasses were brought out with bread and honey. Some of the honey dripped on the outside of the jar. The cans and dishes were washed and put away. The men stored most of their gear on the airplane because they were leaving early in the morning.

During the night, a bear and her two cubs entered their camp. Hugh was the first to awake. He tried his cell phone to warn the two detectives. The curious cubs entered his tent. Hugh covered his head with the sleeping bag and played dead. The cubs found the bag of cinnamon breakfast rolls and ate. Next, they found the opened bag of gummy worms.

Suddenly there was a large roar. The cubs ran out of Hugh's tent. Hugh peered out of his sleeping bag. Loud popping noises went off and hissing sounds of rockets. He heard the boom.

Hugh looked out his tent with gun drawn. He saw Liam and Dodge crawling out the back of their tent with the large sparkler box. They began lighting the sparklers and placing them around the campsite. Dodge approached.

"Glad you are awake; we need the rest of your fireworks."

"Sure."

Hugh scrambled to find his shoes. He exited the tent in time to see the last of the rockets and fireworks blow. The large sparklers were lit around his tent. The entire scene should have scared the mom and babies far from their camp. The whole area was a burst of light and deafening sound.

"Those were the best rockets ever, Hugh."

The three men laughed and found some more firewood to add to the low flame in their firepit. They used a stick to push the empty honey jar into the fire.

"How do you suppose the bear got the cover off the jar?" asked Liam.

"I don't rightly know. Maybe the lid wasn't on tight," mentioned Dodge.

Hugh exclaimed, "Our breakfast is gone and the candy worms. We do have apple juice."

"I vote we turn in for the night. If the bears come back, we shoot toward the woods."

Dodge nodded.

"As long as we don't shoot toward the lake. We don't need holes in the floats. Let's take down Hugh's tent. He should sleep with us."

The three men dismantled the tent, and Hugh moved in. In the morning, they put their rain gear on and took down the second tent. After their gear and garbage were stored, the men jumped inside the floatplane.

18 Return Trip and Landing

Dodge saw the two detectives were safely buckled in their seats. He took off, and the men looked at their campsite on the lake in Washington. The view made them smile. The mother bear and her cubs were playing around their campsite.

"It looks like we left in the nick of time," said Liam.

Hugh took a photograph of the bears and sent a text to his kids.

"The bear cubs found the sour worms in the sand. I guess the bag fell open when we were scrambling to light the fireworks. There was an extra bag, so I emptied them before we left. Those cubs were like children."

The other detectives didn't comment. Hugh acknowledged they were quiet because it was early. The aluminum coffee pot at camp wasn't as good as the expensive coffee machine in the office. He fell asleep.

Dodge and Liam grabbed their sunglasses from the visor.

"I've contacted my friend to let him know when we might arrive. He's put out a red buoy."

Liam wondered about the buoy.

"I understand the small white buoys are the runway guides. The red buoy in the water means what?"

Dodge smiled.

"I accidentally ran into his dock upon landing while we were training. The buoy is to remind me the engine should be cut."

He shook his head in wonder.

"Dodge, sometimes I don't want to know you."

"Isn't that strange? We both agree on one thing. The new dock cost two thousand. We split the difference because I did him a favor. The old dock was rickety."

Liam peered out from his sunglasses.

"Aluminum is expensive nowadays."

Dodge closed his fist. Liam did the same. Both men touched hands.

"Make the new more solid."

Liam looked out the window at the ground. There wasn't a drop of water below, yet the landscape carried its very own beauty.

"Solid is important."

After an hour of flying over California, Dodge handed him the paddle.

"I usually don't turn the engine off until after the red buoy. The floats drag a little bit. You either need to paddle toward or push us away from the dock. It's hard to tell with the wind."

"Why is the paddle so short?"

"You're supposed to stand on the floats with the paddle."

"Oh! Isn't that dangerous?"

Hugh woke up.

"Landing is always dangerous. Good thing they put water rudders on for steering except for the plane now becomes a boat. One way or the other, we'll become a marshmallow on the water with the engine off. Don't drop the paddle, Liam."

When the three men landed and stored the gear in their vehicles, they hugged. Liam was feeling better. His boots were only partly wet. All agreed the camping and fishing trip was a success.

"Hugh, next time no honey or candy," said Dodge.

"I shouldn't have left the cinnamon rolls out. I got hungry and ate one during the night."

Liam and Dodge shook their heads in disbelief.

"You clean the fish, and I'll store the cinnamon rolls on the next trip."

Hugh was happy they weren't mad at him.

"There's going to be one more next time. Brilliant idea."

"Hugh, this is just the beginning of fishing. We need to get away from the job and women on occasion. We'll be better prepared. Call this trip a test run."

"See you guys later."

Dodge and Liam watched as Hugh drove away.

"The good thing was you didn't tell him how scared we were. When that mother bear opened our tent flap, I thought we were going to end up in the lake. Then I remembered bears can swim."

"Yeah, I didn't know bears could unzipper a tent."

"The zipper is my fault. I was hot and pulled the zipper down partway."

Liam put his glasses back on.

"At least you had the where-with-all to find the lighter and light the screaming rocket."

Dodge laughed.

"That was a pure gut reaction on tossing the lit rocket at the bear. I'm glad Hugh warned us about the red box. Also, the rocket pointing away from the tent when she landed active was a long shot. We might have lost a tent. I do have a confession. My gun was out of reach."

Liam's eyes lit up underneath the lenses.

"So was mine."

Dodge patted Liam on the back.

"Next time, we really gotta be prepared."

"We should tell Hugh we knew about the bear," said Liam guiltily.

Dodge looked at his truck.

"We don't want to spoil the last expression on his face."

Liam thought about his friend.

"He did look happy."

Liam watched as Dodge walked away.

He took off his rain gear and stuffed the plastic in his trunk. He found the selfie of the three detectives holding the first three fish they caught. This was the picture he sent to Penelope to let her know their group landed. She would know Liam would be home soon.

He put his gun and gun belt in the front seat of the black sports car within arm's reach. The fishing pole barely fit inside the car and was hanging out the passenger window with a red bobber.

On his way home, he stopped at a traffic light and saw Carter. Carter honked, and Liam waved.

"I guess he saw the fishing pole. I think I'll let Hugh tell the fishing story to the other detectives."

There was no way he was going to tell anyone about the lit flares. He arrived home, and Penelope helped him store his gear in the garage.

"You caught some fish?"

"We did."

She kissed him.

"I missed you, but I'm glad you men had a fun time. Dodge landed okay."

"Missed you more. Hugh snores all the time."

Liam dropped his bag of dirty clothing.

"Dodge texted you that we landed. How did he do that while flying the airplane?"

Penelope looked at Liam's tired eyes.

"He was upon the approach. Was Hugh loud?"

Liam grinned.

"The approach was cool. I was watching the water and the dock. The landing was perfect. We softly bumped the dock. Dodge blamed a wave. As far as the camping trip, Hugh wasn't loud enough to scare the bear. The fireworks did the trick."

Penelope wondered how men still existed in the world.

"Macho trip."

Liam hugged and kissed her welcome lips.

"This was an extreme trip. I've come to the logical conclusion that bears are smart, and Dodge flies by the seat of his pants."

"I thought you men took your guns."

She ignored the comment about Dodge. The man was a professional and could do stunts in the air.

"We did. The mother black bear appeared with her babies."

"Aw, how sweet?"

She went into the kitchen. Liam took his raincoat out. The lighter was in the pocket. He clicked the lighter on and off.

"What did men do without fire?"

Liam shoved the lighter in his barbeque drawer.

"Simple. They were eaten by bears until the women arrived and rubbed two sticks together. Then they stacked the firewood perfectly."

Liam sat on the floor. His wife joined him.

"You and Dodge are a pair of daredevils. I haven't figured out which one is worse. I'll sort your laundry. You can reheat the chili. Emma gave me her cracker recipe. They look like crackers. I was afraid to taste them."

He liked cooking. Frying the fish in foil and pouring lemon juice on top was more than cool at a campsite. He looked at his beach house. The air smelled of hot chili. Liam would pretend to enjoy the crackers.

"Home sweet home."

19 Return Outfit and Jane Beeker

Penelope walked outside the downtown apartment building and selected a cement bench close to a small fountain. She called Liam.

"I'll send you my report on Cathy Blair. In a nutshell, the security guard hasn't seen her in over a month when she and her sister, Jane Beeker, fought. She also hasn't signed up for any classes this semester at the college. Guess what? Her major is avionics, and her minor shows programming. The guard said Cathy sometimes stayed at the Beeker mansion. Paul never mentioned her when we visited."

The message time on her phone ended. She called him back.

"You promised me a new phone. This one has problems. Oh, I'm returning my mom's outfit to the expensive store and should be at the office in about two hours."

Penelope finished her report and sent it to Liam. Next, she drove to the high-end clothing store to return the lounging outfit.

"Hi, my mom decided against this outfit. The color doesn't go with Montana. The charge is on my credit card."

"I do remember you and your mother in the store. Her name was Wendy. I'll check on the price. This tag has been cut in the price spot," said the saleswoman.

"The price is on the receipt, but I don't see the tag number."

"Margo rang up this sale. She forgets to scan all the tags. I should only be a few minutes."

Penelope watched as the woman disappeared to the back of the store. She noticed a woman with beautiful hair moving some hangars. Penelope froze. The woman was Jane Beeker with a bodyguard. She turned back to the counter a distance from the cash register.

Penelope picked up a top that looked interesting. She liked the design and knew the top would work well with blue jean shorts. She found her size. The price was four hundred fifty dollars. Penelope refolded the top and put the item back.

"Detective Knight, I didn't know you shopped here?"

Penelope turned and looked directly at Jane's puzzled look.

"My mother was in town, and we went shopping. I have a lounge outfit to return for her. The color wasn't exactly right for Montana afternoon parties. I'm impressed that you know who I am."

Jane looked slyly at Penelope. Her husband described Penelope Knight to a tee.

"You knew immediately who I was."

Penelope nodded in agreement.

"Your picture was in a magazine article some years ago showcasing your beautiful home. Your hair is the same."

"Aah, yes, those intrusive photographers were unbearable to have in my home. I do like my privacy except when I'm throwing a party. This brings me to my invitation. You and your husband declined. Was there some reason for your absence? Most people accept our invitations."

Penelope glanced and saw the saleswoman returning.

"My husband went to a Northern part of Washington state on a camping and fishing trip with some buddies. I didn't feel right in coming unescorted to your party."

"Pity. Did they catch any fish?"

Penelope laughed.

"They did catch fish. They ate largemouth bass and trout. They ran into a hungrier bear Saturday evening. The honey jar was the trigger, not the cooked fish with lemon."

The saleswoman interrupted.

"I have the correct ticket and will issue your credit."

"Thank you."

Jane's security guard put the hangar of clothes on the counter. Penelope counted three outfits and a tan jacket. Two other women entered the store and looked at the new sweater tops and slacks. Penelope glanced their way. Her attention was redirected to Jane.

"When did your husband go on this fishing trip?"

Penelope wasn't sure why the question was of importance.

"They left early Thursday morning and returned Sunday afternoon. A friend let them borrow a floatplane to land on the lake."

There was a strange look on Jane's face.

"Are you all right? You look ill. Here, let me buy you a water bottle."

Penelope handed Jane the water. The woman opened the container and took two swallows. Jane quickly got control of her emotions.

"The water helped. I thought your husband was following me this week. I guess not. He was at survival camp."

The saleswoman handed Penelope the credit slip. Penelope handed her two dollars for the water. The saleswoman smiled.

"Tell your mom to come to our store the next time she visits. I hear this next year's colors will be more muted. If she opens a charge account, we give twenty percent off your first sales receipt. Our owner has implemented a nice incentive for new customers. Also, we send out discount cards on occasion to the account holders."

"I'll let my mother know. Twenty percent sounds like a deal."

Penelope turned.

"The police were probably following me," said Jane.

"I have no idea. The police don't always coordinate with our department. The person could be anyone. You never know the creeps that are out there. I've run into my fair share on the streets."

Jane looked worried. Penelope needed to leave.

"Have a nice rest of your day. We appreciated the invite. I've heard some gossip that your party was a hit. They mentioned you hired a great band."

The woman didn't respond. Her mind was elsewhere. She snapped back.

"Oh, the band was the Grand Storm Troopers. They are the current popular rock band. My husband certainly enjoyed dancing with his female guests. He broke open the expensive tequila. Five bottles at $2,500 a bottle. Wasteful was my thinking."

Penelope's look of awe encouraged the woman's anger.

"The bartenders stopped him from getting the thirty-thousand-dollar bottle from the wine cellar. The bottle has diamonds embedded on the surface. Well, that felt good to let out a little steam."

"I'll bet. My husband and I argue over the small stuff, too."

Jane smiled wickedly.

"You're interesting."

"You, too."

Penelope left the store with her head held high. She walked to her car. She drove to a coffee shop that she liked. Four silver-lined bags of coffee for Liam and her office were bought. Grabbing the type of coffee that Hugh always liked, she waited while the clerk put them in a larger shopping bag. Putting the package in her car, she thought about the conversation with Jane.

"The odds of running into Jane Beeker were fairly low. Yet, she did. The woman looked afraid for a moment and disappeared on me into her thoughts. The question is why?"

Penelope started her gray sports car.

"She invited us to the party, not Paul. I wonder if he knew we were even on the guest list. I would have liked to see the pricey bottle and grabbed a dance. The Grand Storm Troopers are hot in the local area! Their song, Pink Sky, hits a nerve."

She decided not to tell Liam about the strange meeting with Jane. The party invite and his reaction still bothered her.

"Paul sounds like a party person running close to being a little wild. I bet he doesn't go on fishing trips."

Penelope hummed the song, *Pink Sky*, as she drove to the office. The strange email she received from some creep didn't faze her today. She felt invincible.

"We should do pizza tonight."

Penelope switched radio stations and heard the announcer describe the next song. *Pink Sky* came on. She turned down the volume. Her day was moving in the right direction.

She tried Hugh's phone. She left a message.

"Hugh, what was the name of the pizza place you and Emma like? Send me a text because I'm driving. You mentioned mozzarella cheese, fresh tomato, and basil woodfired. I'm going to the office. The creep sent a third note. I don't care."

Penelope disconnected and turned up the volume on the radio. The song ended when she pulled into the department's parking lot. She was a little late.

"Oh, well, Tim Brewster isn't going anywhere."

20 Simon and Karry

Susan turned in the report for herself and Carter. During the past week, their tasks were to interview the four dead professionals' relatives via conference call and in-person if possible. Liam read the report and went back to one or two interviews.

Per Simon's relatives, he originally received an offer of employment from another company and was contemplating not joining the Beeker Star Ships Company. Simon mentioned a woman who was also considering a job with the same firm but joined the Beeker firm. They didn't know the name of the first company. Simon did mention the other firm was in the Los Angeles area.

No company came forward to the police when the names of the dead were published in the newspaper. The other company didn't need to get involved.

Also, he hadn't spoken with his parents for a year but did send them a letter. There was a short text a few days before his death. Liam knew about the short text. The man said he was going on a tour.

"Simon was going on a tour of what?"

He read the next paragraph. Simon bragged about a new revolutionary design he liked. He did not tell them he was building anything. The man saw a prototype. There was a minor flaw that he believed could be corrected through software.

Liam read the third paragraph of the letter to his parents dated six months previously.

The device acted erratic and pinpointed objects were overshot. The error occurred at random. In other words, the controller lost control. The device seemed to be overtaken by another controller. I'll need to let them know.

"Who did he let know of the glitch, and what was the device? The device has to be a drone."

Liam read the report on Karry Sullivan. Her parents didn't know about her job, or the company she worked for. Their daughter was a stranger to them.

There was even smaller information regarding Blake and Melody Barkley.

"If I were going to hire people whose identities could easily not matter, these four people were the perfect target of some psycho."

Liam remembered the registered drones that were stolen in Roman Manning's warehouse were normal drones.

"What if Simon was working off designs from military-grade drones used for swarm warfare. Pinpointing the target would be crucial for selling to high-priced bidders. Where would he get the military-grade designs? Steal a military drone would be my guess. The only problem was the software, or the controller didn't work. Maybe a new software app has better capability than the ground station controller. The drone as a deterrence was a bust on the first one of the prototypes."

He contemplated his next move.

"Were the four people killed because they failed, or did they finally fix the problem and were disposable? Again, who was their employer? The

Beeker company employed them. Were they working with another firm after hours to build a freaking flying computer?"

Liam went into his boss's office. They needed to see where and when any military-grade small drones or designs were stolen. Also, were there any new apps using sophisticated software that could cause a drone to go haywire.

After he met with his boss, Liam drove to the store and purchased waterproof phones for his team. He wanted to be sure they could always call into the office.

Liam checked his mail and saw his wife had received a third harassment note. He looked at the date and time. The note came in an hour ago. He called Tim Brewster.

"Tim, this person is raising the bar on this note. This is the third one. Tell me you have something."

"The person is good at hiding. We're installing a new trap on her computer when she returns to the office. Sometimes we get one step ahead of them. Penelope told me she is twelve minutes out. She asked that I install the software in person rather than electronically."

Liam looked at the ceiling.

"Make this trap work. I don't want any of my detectives bothered by some idiot with a computer."

"Yes, sir."

His cell phone rang.

"Dodge, I didn't get your report."

"Liam, some of us are busy doing our job and everybody else's. Hugh's phone battery quit. I told him to call you first. Of course, he doesn't follow my orders.

Therefore, I called to warn you about the phone exchange.

"I'll call him. Everyone is getting new waterproof phones."

Liam stopped. "I can't call him."

"About Davidson and my report, the white vans are back at the warehouse after the party. They washed and buffed them well. The sun sparkling on the hood hurts my eyes. They should have picked black vans. The buyer isn't too bright. I overheard one of the drivers talking about the ship's arrival. The ship we want has arrived and is anchored offshore. She's awaiting Customs and Immigration authorization to dock. He complained about lots of ships were ahead of her. Do you know of anyone who could speed the process? Or should I order pizza this evening?"

Liam chuckled.

"Go order your pizza. You might want to skip the anchovies. I hear there was a worm infestation. The officials on land move slow. I'll drop your phones off at Davidson's house. Thanks for the update."

"No problem. Worms in oil might be tasty. Getting back to the current situation, I can hardly wait to see Hugh's face when he must return that new phone. He bought the phone around Venice Beach. Let's hope he hasn't put duct tape on the outside, or the store hasn't gone out of business."

Liam heard Hugh arrive. He sauntered out to Hugh's desk with the three boxed cell phones.

"Everyone on the team gets a new waterproof phone. The address of the store we want people to use to download their data is taped on the box top. Deliver

Susan and Carter their phone. I'll take care of Dodge, Davidson, and Penelope."

Liam grabbed the last three phone boxes, locked his office, and went in the direction of Tim Brewster's office.

He heard Hugh complaining as he left.

"I heard that."

Hugh listened to his messages on his new phone before he needed to switch phones. He texted Penelope.

"A third note from the creep is not good. Try Maggie's Pizza on 24th Ave."

Hugh sent her a second text with the pizza place phone number.

21 Ship Arrival and Drone Attacker

The dock men were waiting for the ship, Star Caroline II, to arrive at the dock for unloading in the Port of Los Angeles. When no ship arrived, they left for the day and would return the next day. They got paid whether they worked or waited.

Paul Beeker was in contact with the company's Captain Kale Dunkin.

"We made too good a time for our travel from Mexico. The ocean was calm most of the trip. We are used to waiting. The ship is secure until we dock. We checked for stowaways and found none."

"Good. The shipment of tequila this time contains fifty bottles of the expensive stuff. I already have clients waiting for their cases."

"I'll make sure your shipment is safe. There will be no accidents. Our workers appreciated the bonus. The truck drivers are waiting," said Dunkin.

Liam received his second email regarding the ship's arrival. This last email was a note from Paul Beeker.

"The man followed through. He let me know the ship has arrived. I believe the owner wants things to go smoothly with this cargo. I'm sure there is more than fruit on board."

Liam looked at the General Stowage Plan submitted by the company's central planners. Each container's contents, dimensions, and weight were shown. The heavier containers were below deck. He noted the hatch covers so more containers could be stacked in layers above the cover. He saw the food and meat containers. This ship wasn't carrying any automobiles. Most were transported on car tankers which made for more efficiency.

Their interest would be in the specialty containers. He let Dodge and Davidson know. In talking with Dodge, Liam found there was a problem with the ship's paperwork. There would be a holdup in Customs.

"I'm telling you that I overheard the warehouse foreman talking with someone. They mentioned there was disagreement on the duty and taxes. The report filed is not what type of liquor was loaded. Plus, they were supposed to indicate the change in the city to pick up the liquor. There's a new guy that didn't do his job very well. I imagine he won't have a job for long."

"Paul Beeker will correct the reports I'm sure. If not, he will get his lawyer, Rauf Merk involved. For now, we are in a watch-and-wait type mode. We believe the drone parts may be in one of the specialty containers."

"I hope your guess is correct. I would imagine they would place the container near the top of the ship and park it someplace where they wouldn't need to re-stow the box when they dropped other containers off in San Diego. Let's hope the Customs people don't find a worker smoking weed, or they'll seize the entire ship," said Dodge.

Liam could always count on Dodge to scare the heck out of a person.

"I'd sure hate to wait another thirty days. My boss is waving at me. If anything pops, call me back."

Dodge saw Davidson waving at him. "Aren't you glad I pay attention? Davidson is here to relieve the dog."

"Yes, I am. Keep up the good work."

Liam went into his boss's office. Jonathan appeared to be in a jovial mood.

"We have some good news. The police have arrested a man flying a drone near one of the remote beaches. The drone isn't registered. When they looked on his car seat, they found a notebook."

Liam grinned appreciatively.

"Don't tell me. The guy recorded the day, the time, the distance the drone flew, and the location of his escapades."

"There is a match to your wife's report of the drone at your condominium. The man, Shep Lipton, will be charged for that misguided drone attack on a human being. We're looking into the other ten flights from his notebook."

"I'd like a crack at talking to the man."

Jonathan already grabbed Carter because Liam was busy with the tanker.

"Carter has left and will visit the jail to interview the man. I want you to stay on the tanker. I understand Customs has a slight problem. Immigration will wait until they are done before they clear the ship. I imagine the workers will get ugly if things take too long."

Liam nodded. He would follow orders, and let Carter handle the jail interview.

"Paul told me he pays the ship workers for their time. The workers probably won't mind the delay. What if we are wrong about the drone parts?"

Jonathan was worried, too.

"We do know something is wrong in the Beeker Company. Four of their workers died mysteriously, and bodies were deposited in a warehouse containing a drug lab. We have possible scenarios. Paul Beeker is guilty, someone is using his company, or he's the target in someone's scope. Our job is to figure out which one of the scenarios is true. The drone theory makes sense because of the education and training of the dead people. If we are wrong, we move to Plan B."

"What is our Plan B and C?"

"Plan B is that Roman Manning and Benny Lourdes are up to something. We doubt that Benny will try the illegal import of salvage cars in whole or parts. Then there's the drug lab Manning says he didn't know about."

Liam was sure of Manning's guilt. The man was always nervous. He smoked up a storm around Lourdes.

"Plan C is that Jane Beeker and Rauf Merk seem a little too cozy when Paul's not around. Plus, she works in the Human Resource Department and withheld three of the victim's Visa extension requests. She said she forgot and went on vacation. We doubt this woman forgets anything which brings us right back to Paul. He okayed Simon to work for his firm."

Liam also summarized the problem in his head. The two men thought alike.

"The police we stationed around the Beeker's last Friday recorded Manning and Lourdes's cars at a gas station within two miles of the Beeker party," commented Liam.

"Bears congregate around a honey pot."

Liam laughed.

"Stick with the plan for now. If things change, we can move in another direction. The Chief has given us his support."

The lead detective was glad there were other plans. The Chief wanted the criminals caught no matter how long things took.

"If things take longer than we expect, I'll need to relieve Dodge and Davidson for a couple of days."

Jonathan watched Liam.

"Penelope and I can step in."

"Hugh is also available if you want to leave Penelope out. This case may be more dangerous than the last. The undercover police we have stationed around the Beeker's housing community haven't seen Jane's sister, Cathy Blair. There's also been a strange development."

Liam's head jerked.

"What strange development?"

Jonathan tapped his ink pen on a pad.

"We're not the only ones investigating the Beeker's besides Drug Enforcement."

Liam wondered about the other agencies. Any one of them could step into the investigation. If the parts were exact copies of the military drones, the big guns would take over.

"The federal government is also involved."

"I wish that were the case. The undercover police have seen a few mob members driving around in the city following someone. We have no idea who hired them. There also was a strange car with no plates that got away."

Liam was startled when his boss gave him the information.

"Two women followed Jane into the same high-end store your wife went to last week."

"Penelope and Jane were in the same store at the same time."

Jonathan slid two photographs showing Jane and Penelope in conversation from the outside of the store. They were standing together inside next to a cash register. Liam shook his head. He remembered his wife's conversation.

"She returned an outfit her mother purchased."

The Captain stood and opened his door.

"She didn't put the meeting in her report. You might need to discuss the omission with your detective."

Liam knew he was being dismissed. He walked to his office and waited for Penelope to return. He buzzed her to come into his office.

She came in and sat down. He told her about the drone operator and then shoved the two photographs at her.

"Revise your report. I'm going home. Pull the door shut when you leave."

Liam left her alone.

When she returned home to Liam's house, she changed and jogged to the beach. She found her husband sitting.

She squatted.

"The Captain knows that I messed up?"

"He doesn't miss much although your husband certainly does."

"I'm sorry. It won't happen again. The report has been corrected. I will apologize to our Captain tomorrow."

She stood, and he watched her jog away.

Liam knew she shouldn't run alone. He jogged after her.

22 Penelope's Apology

Penelope waited for the Captain to finish his phone conversation. He concluded his call.

"Detective Knight, I imagine you are here to apologize for the photographs I gave to your supervisor."

Penelope bit her lip and straightened her jacket.

"I do apologize. I should have mentioned the meeting about accidentally running into Jane Beeker."

Jonathan noted that she offered no excuses for her error in judgment.

"We all slip on occasion. Make sure we always have the complete report. Even the littlest things can be hugely important, especially in a complicated case such as this one."

"Yes, sir."

Jonathan liked Penelope. She had a fire in her belly and spoke her mind. As a detective, she was almost as good as her husband. Then he thought about what his brain fired back.

"Overall, you are one of my best detectives. I value your opinion as much as the others. If there is a problem, you can count on me being fair."

Penelope liked Jonathan, too.

"Thank you for saying nice things. The warning has been softened because I'm still considered a rookie."

Jonathan shoved back his chair. He settled into a comfortable position. His detective relaxed.

"You aren't a rookie in my book. Tell me your thoughts regarding Jane Beeker. You are probably the only one of our detectives to get within ten miles of her. Usually, her security people block our path."

"The woman is beautiful, older, sophisticated, and intelligent."

"Those are admirable outer qualities everyone sees. I'm talking about your first instincts. Give me the gut reaction to meeting an extraordinarily rich and powerful woman."

Penelope knew where Jonathan was going.

"Deadly, sir."

He didn't laugh or smile.

"I met Jane about five years ago at a city social function. My gut reaction then was the same as yours now. We might want to revise the phrase to *more deadly*. She has had plenty of time to grow."

Penelope remembered how upset Liam was about her nondisclosure about meeting Jane Beeker.

"Liam was furious."

Jonathan felt sympathy for the newlywed couple. They weren't into the groove of married detective life.

"He will get over his anger. In the meantime, I'd like to know if you would be up to digging a little deeper into Cathy Blair's disappearance. There is something fishy that has happened. I'm wondering who the woman is hiding from. I'm guessing the person is her sister."

Penelope remembered the major and minor the woman was taking in college.

"You think Cathy knows what happened to the four dead people."

Now Jonathan smiled.

"I think she might."

Penelope couldn't see that her husband entered his office and saw the two of them talking together.

"If your idea were true, Cathy may be in grave danger. She does have money. Money may be considered support. Once support isn't required, she might be an object in the way."

Jonathan put his fingers together in a familiar steeple fashion. Penelope's brain raced.

"If she's in danger, someone is looking for her. This someone could be Jane or a person much deadlier."

Jonathan blew on his fingers.

"Give this detective a prize."

Penelope knew her boss played her.

"What do I tell Liam?"

He nodded. "Tell him that I have given you an assignment. Research is always important to the case."

"If I get into trouble?"

Jonathan saw Hugh enter Liam's office.

"Take Hugh with you when you talk with anyone outside this office. Make sure you have plenty of bullets. That will be all today detective."

23 Marvin's Fern

Penelope went to her desk and was delighted to see Susan Clemens.

"Hi, Carter went to the doctor. His hand is finally fine. We went to the gun range, and he was able to shoot and hit the target. I wanted you to know."

"I appreciate the information."

Susan watched as Penelope checked the work schedule.

"Our Captain told me to make sure I checked with you on occasion. I'm good at research."

Penelope remembered some students at Cathy's school.

"I do have some college student's names and phone numbers. I'm trying to find Cathy Blair, Jane Beeker's sister. I would like to ask her a few questions. The time has been crazy, and I never made the call to them."

Susan mentioned, "I have some free time this afternoon. Why don't I finish the phone calls? I used to attend the college Cathy attended. I know some of her teachers."

Penelope was pleased with the news. The student might have talked to her professors on occasion. The idea was a good one. She forgot how some colleges fostered their students and were like family.

"When you get done, we can get together to discuss your findings. Then you can submit your report to Liam."

Susan left, and Penelope relaxed until her husband appeared.

"You talked with Jonathan?"

"Everything is settled. He would like me to research Ms. Blair. Susan used to attend the same college and will help."

"Fine. I'm going to the shooting range with Hugh and Carter. We want to make sure he can shoot with real bullets."

Penelope turned around to her computer and started typing.

Liam knew their disagreement the prior evening still disturbed her. He sat on her desk. She stopped typing.

"Stop shutting me off."

Penelope wasn't shutting him off.

"I'm trying to work."

"You know what I mean."

A man approached and Liam stood. Penelope smiled.

"Marvin, how nice to see you. We thought you were avoiding us. You brought me a tiny fern. The plant is lovely."

"Mr. Edmond, our District Attorney. I heard that you and your wife were back together. Congratulations."

Mr. Edmond looked angry and his face reddened.

“As of yesterday, we are not and I repeat, not together.”

Mr. Edmond looked at Penelope.

“This plant talked to me. You were my first thought when I saw the fern in the flower shop. I told myself you would love another one to hide from your boss.”

Penelope touched the fern leaves tenderly which made her husband cringe.

“I’m sorry to hear the sad news about your marriage. Hugh and Carter are waiting for me. We’re going to shoot something to keep the adrenaline going. More ferns will give this office a nice shot of green. I’ll make sure my wife remembers to water the plant. She sometimes forgets things.”

Marvin sat down in Penelope’s chair as Liam looked back. He walked out the back door of the building and slammed it shut hard. The door banged loudly.

“What is with your husband?”

Penelope spread her hands out and toyed with a strand of loose hair.

“Bad day, I guess.”

Marvin talked with Penelope for thirty minutes before Jonathan rescued her.

“Hello, Marvin, come into my office. I can update you on a drone attacker who is currently in jail.”

24 Tim's Fault

Penelope stared at the fern. She knew the plant irritated Liam more than seeing a man she dated a couple of times in the past.

"This day is already in the toilet."

Kamilla, the day scheduler, stopped by her desk to chat.

"Since you detectives are on this case, I never get to see anyone. My list of birthday cakes to make has diminished."

"I'm sorry. We have been busy. Someday we'll have a cake day. I think our detectives should make cakes."

Kamilla found the cake day idea interesting seeing as how Detective Knight never made a boxed cake or a boxed frosting.

"I would like the cake day even more. Your idea is excellent. There is a reason for my visit. Jonathan's secretary and I talk on occasion. She is sweet and doesn't gossip, but she controls this office."

Penelope knew about Jonathan's bright and sociable secretary. Kamilla ignored the detective now she was on a roll.

"However, she did mention a little problem you were having at work. I decided because I've worked here longer, you need my support and guidance. We should put our heads together."

Penelope could count on her hands the number of problems.

"Which little problem were you thinking?"

"I hear you have received three harassment email notes. This is terrible news but don't let anyone scare you. We, women, stick together. Buy yourself some mace. The fern is new and rather cute. I assume Mr. Edmond is visiting."

"Yes, he is with our boss. Jonathan was waiting for him. I have received some notes from a real jerk and computer creep. I do carry mace. Unfortunately, the mace won't go over electric wires or the internet. Tim Brewster is following the notes."

Penelope showed her the emails.

"This is strange. The words look familiar. The person repeats himself. The other person did, too."

Penelope suddenly was wide awake.

"Explain strange and familiar to me. I caught the repeats in the notes."

Kamilla glanced around the room. She whispered.

"You don't have any bugs in this room?"

Penelope shook her head.

"I doubt Jonathan would allow them."

"About two years ago, one of the other female detectives received similar notes. Jonathan was on an extended vacation, and the reports went directly to the Chief."

"I wasn't a detective at this office two years ago," said Penelope.

"Tim never found the person. Everyone says he is good with computers. The word genius gets thrown around. So, why didn't he find the person who sent the notes?"

Kamilla gave her the prior detective's name and approximate periods the notes were received.

"Thank you. I'm going to mention what you told me to my boss. Don't discuss this with anyone except Jonathan."

Kamilla left, and Penelope went into her boss's office. Marvin was gone. He told her there was another agency he would call. The investigation would begin.

Penelope looked at the time and walked to the deli. She ordered half a tuna salad sandwich with a cup of tomato soup. It wasn't long before Liam joined her with a roast beef sandwich order. He selected them each a cola.

"I decided today wasn't a good day to go shooting. I made Hugh return me to the office. I acted a little strange seeing the plant and the DA."

"Your reaction was bad."

Liam took a large bite of his sandwich. He put the sandwich down.

"I love you, and sometimes I get carried away."

"I know you love me. We love each other too much."

He stopped.

"Eat your sandwich. You'll feel better."

Liam finished his sandwich. "Your tomato soup looks good."

She passed him the cup.

"Jonathan asked that I tell you something in confidence."

Liam finished the soup.

"Tim Brewster sent the notes."

"Yes, how did you know? I mean we don't know, but there is a quiet investigation started."

"I remembered the other female detective when Hugh was driving me back. She reported to Davidson. He briefly mentioned the emails. I'm glad they will investigate."

"Tim's career will be over in law enforcement."

Liam nodded.

"If he is found guilty, Tim will be charged with felony crimes and more than likely, wire fraud."

She swirled her ice.

"Tim didn't try to extract money from me."

Liam watched his wife's face.

"He can be charged with wire fraud if he accessed your personal and confidential information. We believe he did."

Penelope watched as her husband threw their garbage away.

"There's a short walk down the street where a man makes these dainty cookies. You look like you could use a high dose of fructose. Shall we take a stroll?"

Penelope took Liam's hand. She knew cookies weren't very nutritious, but she wanted something sweet.

"I thought we could buy a couple dozen for the office. Hugh looked like he could use some sugar, too."

They selected four dozen different flavors of cookies. The new owner threw in six cookies extra, and they ate six in the store while tasting.

When they reached the office, Penelope asked, "What should I do with the plant?"

Liam took the tiny fern plant and deposited the plant firmly on Hugh's desk with a small box of cookies for his family. He pretended to dust the dirt off his hands.

"Emma gets a new fern today and dessert."

Penelope was all right with the gifts.

"We should invite everyone over sometime soon for burgers and brats. The tile workers have completed our back patio at the beach house. You men can cook."

Liam knew they needed to return to work. They walked to their office.

Penelope turned on her computer and began checking Cathy's tax records. There was no income reported.

"Who paid your rent, food, and clothing?"

She contacted the apartment manager.

"The Beeker Star Ships Company paid Cathy's bills for the last three years since her arrival from Hong Kong. I saw Mrs. Beeker give her the checks."

Penelope thanked the man.

"The woman went to college for three years and dropped out. They more than likely paid for her college expenses."

Penelope was stuck. She looked at the empty desks in the office. She knew where each detective went.

"Does Jane know where Cathy is located? I could call her. Not a good idea. I would look like a detective following a lead, and she wouldn't be friendly."

Susan slid in Penelope's chair.

"I have news. None of her college friends have heard from Cathy. They wondered if she returned to Hong Kong. Her sister kept threatening to send her there. They fought over the money things were costing and Cathy's weird friends."

There was a moment of defeat. Penelope took her eraser and threw it in the garbage.

"I could never figure out why they gave us erasers. We have computers."

Susan raised her hand.

"Can I have your eraser?"

Penelope dug the eraser from the garbage and handed the pink rubber to Susan.

"I'm frustrated."

Susan put the eraser in her purse.

"They did tell me Cathy was acting strangely the week before she disappeared. She was going to find some answers about the products. She was taking a tour."

Penelope's head raised.

"Simon Needham told his parents he was going on a tour. The tour probably wasn't one in Oregon where the four were going on vacation. The odds are the tour was somewhere in LA. Cathy knew about the tour. I wonder."

"The tour might be where everyone died," suggested Susan.

"I think you might be correct. We need to find the person who holds the key, so we can unravel this mess."

Susan frowned.

"You think one person is responsible?"

Penelope pondered the question.

"In my world, there's usually someone that seems the likely culprit."

Susan was getting the picture.

"We're looking for the stranger."

"Exactly."

The two female detectives acknowledged they were looking for the same clue.

"I heard Hugh went to gun practice with Carter. He called me and complained."

"Hugh likes to shoot his gun. The noise from home gets too much. He enjoys the heavy-duty headphones at the gun range. I'm sure he wanted company is all."

The two women heard the racket in the hall.

"The gun-toting warriors have returned. The cookies ought to sweeten their day. I'll help you write your report."

The two women finished the report and sent it off to Liam. Penelope would submit hers later. They joined the men detectives in the bullpen area. Hugh took Penelope aside.

"Marvin was here today!"

Penelope hissed.

"Be quiet. I don't want anyone to know. Everyone remembers the flowers in the garbage."

"That's why your husband made me drive back?"

Penelope rolled her eyes.

"The cookies are good. There's a new bakery down the street. I met the man the other day and gave Liam the heads up. He told me his mom made cookies when he was young. Emma thanks you for the fern and sweets."

"Marvin's divorce is on again."

"Oh, good grief, no. We must keep him away from Susan," said Hugh.

"I agree wholeheartedly. A relationship is unpredictable with Marvin. However, it would serve Carter right. He takes advantage of Susan's good nature. She's always turning in the reports."

Hugh got a mischievous look on his face. He hollered, so everyone in the office heard.

"Hey, Carter, next time you write and turn in the report to Liam."

Carter swallowed and whispered.

"Is that why he was so mad today?"

"Beats me. I only work here."

Hugh picked up his briefcase, plant, and box of cookies. He strolled away.

"See you, everyone."

A few of the detectives waved. Hugh winked at Susan and Penelope.

25 Carter Visits Drone Attacker

Carter walked with the Jailer to Shep Lipton's jail cell. He took out his list of questions to ask the man. The prisoner used an illegal small drone to scare and attack people. The questions were specifically from Liam because the man used a drone to scare Penelope at their condominium in Los Angeles.

The door was unlocked, Carter stepped inside, and the Jailer waited outside the bars. The man sat on his bunk bed and didn't move.

"I'm with the Los Angeles Detective Unit, and you can call me Carter. You have been arrested because the drone is illegal, and you pursued people with the device. Those people are pretty upset and felt their lives were threatened by you. There are some questions about the specific drone that you had in your possession. The device seems to be a stolen prototype."

The man in green and white coveralls shuffled his feet on the cold cement floor.

"The cat told me you would come. I didn't believe it."

Carter blinked and hesitated. He cleared his throat.

"We would like to know where you found the drone or tell us about the person who gave you the device?"

"You were right the first time," said Lipton.

Carter corrected his question.

"Tell us from whom you stole the drone."

Lipton looked at the Jailer.

"Make him disappear, and I'll tell you."

Carter nodded for the Jailer to give them six feet.

"He hasn't disappeared."

Carter was getting upset at the person in the jail clothes.

"I'm here to offer you a deal. You let us know from whom you stole the drone, and we can make your life a little more comfortable."

The man snorted.

"Comfortable is the best you can do. Your comfortable means real hamburger and baby shampoo. No thanks. Besides, someone beat you to the punchline. They've offered me a way out. I'm being taken care of with a better plan."

Carter wasn't sure who the man was talking about because the Jailer told him the man received no visitors. He tried another tactic.

"This drone is special. The device was built by a group of very bright people. Those people we assume are now dead."

The man wasn't affected by the statement.

"At least they don't have any more worries."

The Jailer let Carter know he had five minutes.

"We need to know how you obtained the drone you have. It is critical in helping us catch the criminals."

The prisoner looked at Carter.

"You have no idea the people who you are messing around with."

Carter looked at the prisoner in the eye.

"You'll go down with them."

"Maybe and maybe not," quipped Lipton.

The prisoner rubbed his nose. Carter turned to let the Jailer know he was done with his interview.

Suddenly the prisoner fell over and started convulsing. Carter jumped back grabbing the bars. The Jailer opened the door and called for someone on his radio. Carter backed out of the cell and froze against the wall.

Guards rushed into the cell. They checked the man's pulse and shook their head. Carter blinked and came back from wherever he went.

"Lipton's dead?"

"I'm afraid he is very dead. His lips are turning blue. I'd say a possible substance of some kind."

"Do you need me to complete any papers?" asked Carter.

"No, Harvey witnessed the whole thing. He's all we need. You can go."

Carter went to his vehicle and climbed inside. He called Liam and told him what happened.

"You can send me your report tomorrow."

"It was unreal. He was shaking violently."

"I understand. This isn't the first time that criminals have taken someone out while in jail. I didn't think they would work this fast," said Liam.

"I should have talked to the man longer."

Carter shook his head still in disbelief at the turn of events.

"The guy was committed to die the minute he was caught. He knew the drone idea was deep trouble. I just wish he would have given us a clue where he stole the device. He talked about a cat and that's the only name he used."

"Go home, Carter. There isn't anything more we can do about Lipton. He has no relatives nor friends that we can find. The man was a bum, and he was living on the streets. He could have found the drone in a dumpster. We assumed there was only one prototype. There could have been many more. We'll let our boys take the drone apart."

"I'm driving home after I stop at the grocery store and buy something frozen. There shouldn't be anything dangerous in frozen food."

Liam knew Carter didn't cook.

"Tell you what. I have a chef friend who makes great spaghetti meals with homemade French bread. Go home, and I'll have his delivery guy bring you a decent meal. Look for a truck with Johnny's on the side. It is the least I can do to help calm the frayed nerves."

"Thanks, Liam. I am fried and ragged."

Liam rang off and called the restaurant. After ordering a dinner size meal and paying for the food, he drove home.

Penelope greeted him at the laundry room door. He shook his head. She shut the door and went into the kitchen.

"I fixed us some salad. There are some pork chops we can fry or barbeque."

Liam went outside to start the grill. Penelope followed.

"Lipton took some poison during Carter's interview. No one knows how he obtained the small plastic vial. He believed the person who gave him the drug was offering him a joyride and a trip to a hospital where he might have a better chance to escape. He was wrong."

"Is Carter safely at home?"

"I ordered him a spaghetti meal from Johnny's."

Penelope handed him the plate with the pork chops. She went inside.

Her husband was alone to be with his thoughts and cook.

26 Helicopter Ride

Saturday Dodge and Liam went to the hangar where Dodge stored his helicopter.

"I purchased a camera for the chopper so we can take good aerial pictures of the warehouse complex in Los Angeles."

"Great. I can hardly wait to see the views."

They flew over the warehouse Dodge and Davidson were currently watching. The ten white trucks looked like sentinels on the ground. The burned warehouse was gone. Graders smoothed new sand and cement trucks poured a slab the same size as the old one. Liam ran the camera after Dodge told him how to move the lens and the buttons to push.

"Try moving Northward and fly in a large circle. If there's a specific area, I'll zoom the lens closer."

Dodge complied. Liam pointed at a grouping of three warehouses. Dodge maneuvered and flew over the buildings. The helicopter turned and flew a distance further away.

"We should get closer."

"Two vehicles are approaching the three building's zone. I'm going to fly further away, so they don't get suspicious. We can come back in five minutes. The vehicles should still be there, and the men should be inside the warehouse. Be ready to shoot hot and heavy. Get any licenses if you can."

"Did you notice the same white vans? I counted ten."

Dodge looked at the sky for any air traffic.

"It was nice of the car dealer to call me. His friend down the street received the order for the vans. The man bragged about how much money he made because the man was in a rush to buy. He happened to have six on his lot and four more at his second dealership in Oakland."

They flew over the three warehouse complex a second time, and Liam took pictures.

"I think we have enough. Put the bird down. We can go to the office to review the photos. Jonathan is waiting. I'm glad Carter could stay with Davidson today."

"Too bad about young Lipton," said Dodge.

Liam sighed, "He was disposable. We also know there is someone on the force who inadvertently let slip we caught Lipton. Lipton might have been given the drones for disposal in exchange for drugs. Unfortunately for Lipton, he decided to keep one for his sick enjoyment. Bad move."

Dodge showed Liam how to transfer the photos to his cell phone. They went to the office.

"Hello, Dodge. I knew you thought this weekend was going to be time off. When you called Liam about the second batch of vans, we needed to get a better look."

"No problem. I like flying the chopper on the weekend with my dog. He was upset we didn't take him. We'll go up tomorrow. The dog likes egg sandwiches."

Jonathan chuckled and took out a twenty-dollar bill. He handed the bill to Dodge.

"My treat for tomorrow."

Liam hooked his camera to the viewer's device. Jonathan pulled down the large screen. Taking the clicker, the men looked at the photos. They stopped at a couple of screens. Jonathan wrote down license plate numbers and made a phone call.

"Gentlemen, we have a second warehouse leased by Lourdes."

Dodge looked at Liam.

"We've been taken for a ride. Lourdes has gotten a little cleverer since he went to prison. Manning should have steered clear of the man."

Liam put the remote next to the viewer machine after turning off the device. Jonathan pushed the button, so the screen retracted.

"Put Hugh and Carter on the second warehouse until Drug Enforcement arrives," ordered Jonathan.

Liam stepped out to make the call.

"Shoot, my boxes in the warehouse I'm watching are the duds. I was hoping to make a big splash in helping find drugs."

"Don't worry Dodge, the drug boys will be delighted. They know you've been patiently waiting. I'll let them know to give you a call when they have the goods and suspects in hand."

Liam stepped into the office.

"Hugh is on his way to get Carter. His wife has packed them lunch and coffee."

"Good work today."

Dodge and Liam left the office and walked to the parking lot.

"Where's your sweet wife?"

"She went shopping for makeup at the mall. The color she ordered online is the wrong one. I don't expect her back anytime soon."

"The malls aren't what they used to be. Older kids are stealing more and more. Graffiti is written on the bathroom stalls. My thoughts are that it is a real shame and a disgrace to write bad words. Why don't they go home and write on their walls? Their mamas would take the heavy frying pan to their heads and the lid to their hands. They would be lucky if she weren't cooking at the time."

It was Liam's turn to chuckle. He hadn't thought much about shopping malls. Dodge continued his tirade.

"The stores are closing shop. The malls have become a wasteland. It's safer to run the business store from a warehouse. People also like to order online from the comfort of their homes. There is a downside for the consumer. No touching makes a person order more."

"I guess we have our vices like fishing stores."

"Don't ruin my day, Liam. I need to touch those lures and rods. You must pick the right green lure. Did you know there are about thirty different types of green?"

Liam visualized his tackle box.

"At least the plastic worms are the correct color range, red to purplish."

"Not anymore."

Liam grinned.

"Well, it's a good thing fish aren't colorblind. I'm sticking with the red to purplish worms with a little cottage cheese added for flavor."

Dodge looked at him strangely.

"Is that what the cottage cheese in our cooler was for? Sorry, I ate half the container. See, I learned something today."

27 Shopping Trip

Penelope took her bag of makeup and stood in the line for a salad and shake at the mall's food court. A man approached behind her.

"Penelope, I didn't know you liked to shop here."

"Marvin. What a nice surprise! This mall carries the makeup brand that I like to wear. I decided to grab some food. Liam is busy having fun with Dodge in his helicopter."

Marvin held up his shopping bag containing two boxes of shoes.

"They carry my favorite brand of shoes. We'll both order and eat lunch together. There are plenty of tables inside or outside."

"I prefer inside."

"We'll eat inside."

He pointed to a quiet area near a bronze heron statue.

Penelope took her food order and went to the table. Marvin joined her. They ate in silence. Penelope slurped the last of her shake.

"You drink the tequila that Paul Beeker brings from Mexico."

"I do. He usually orders me a case once a year. I buy the cheaper stuff. This time, I did order one of the $3,500 bottles. I was going to give the bottle to my wife. That idea was thrown out the window."

Penelope scrunched up her napkin.

"I heard there was a mix-up in the order when the ship pulled into port for Customs."

Marvin stirred cream in his coffee.

"Oh, there was a huge error."

"I hope Beeker's man didn't get fired."

"Beeker's man was correct. The shipment only contained the cheaper bottles of tequila. The expensive bottles were never loaded from the distillery onto the ship. The error was with one of the manufacturer's people. I'm sure Paul will have the shipment travel on the Star Magnetic. She's been fully repaired in San Diego and is being loaded with containers from Los Angeles."

"Why would they reload the containers? Isn't that expensive?"

Marvin looked at the heron.

"Goods are moved from ship to ship all the time. It's fairly easy to change the destination of goods."

Penelope went to get them a cup of water.

"I heard the bottles come in crates and packing from the distillery. You must have lots of pretty crates in your garage."

"Oh, no. The crates are unpacked at the Beeker warehouse in Long Beach. The warehouse is small. I'm sure Jonathan doesn't know about the place."

"Do you have the address?"

Marvin told her the address. She input the address on her notepad on her phone.

"So, they take the wood crates to this warehouse, unpack the bottles, and then they are delivered in some other packaging."

"The bottles are placed in velvet pouches and put in a disposal plastic carrier. The wood crates and straw-like packing are returned to the distillery for reuse."

Penelope contemplated the picture.

"The wood crate and straw can withstand the cool temperature in the refrigerated container."

"Very good. Only this time, the Star Magnetic will bring the tequila in a twenty-foot container which seems a waste of space. I imagine they will fill the space with the much cheaper tequila bottles. The cheaper bottles are placed in the standard liquor boxes. Paul Beeker is a smart businessman and will flood the market with the cheaper tequila for the summer crowd."

Penelope watched a little girl climb out of her stroller and hug the heron statue.

"Hi, isn't the statue pretty? The size is correct to the one in the wild."

The little girl smiled and ran to her mother.

Marvin slowly smiled.

"You would make a good mom. Sometimes I wish we could have a rerun of our pool date. I'm thinking of letting my wife have the Malibu house. There's a smaller house down the street that I've put an offer on. My real estate agents believe the buyers will take my offer."

"How wonderful? I hope you get a smaller house in the same area."

"I was a little crazy there for some time. You should have hit me over the head."

Penelope didn't know what to say.

"Tell me about this Detective Susan Clemens person."

Penelope stared at Marvin. He saw her look and complained.

"She's only two years younger than you."

"That's exactly the problem. Good day, Marvin. Thanks for lunch and the insight into tequila. I won't give you any information regarding Susan. You are on your own."

"Good seeing you today."

Penelope grabbed her shopping bag and left the mall. When she reached home, Liam was doing laundry. He saw her one package.

"There's more in the trunk."

She shook her head in the negative.

"I ran into Marvin at the mall. We did lunch together."

Liam stopped folding his undershirt and frowned. She hugged him.

"If you get mad, I won't tell you what I found out."

Liam put the shirt on the pile in the laundry bin and carried the plastic bin into the kitchen. He gently put down the bin.

"See, there isn't a mad bone in my body."

"For the moment, there isn't."

"All right, there was a tiny twinge. You met by accident."

She unpacked her makeup. She told him about the small warehouse and the packing crates.

"He verified that there was a mix-up with the expensive tequila."

"An error could have consequences," said Liam.

He told her about Dodge's camera shots. She wasn't surprised by the small warehouse.

"The Drug Enforcement people are in place?"

"They have arrived about five minutes ago. Hugh and Carter are relieved. Hugh invited Carter and Susan over for a casual cookout."

"That was nice of Hugh. We have the best of friends. Oh, Marvin, might buy a smaller house in Malibu, and he asked about Susan."

Liam couldn't believe her.

"Isn't she young for him?"

"She's two years my junior."

Liam kissed his wife on the lips.

"I didn't know you were that old."

She turned to unpackage her makeup.

He hugged her anyway.

"I'm glad you are back. I see you are busy. I'll go to the living room and read my emails and reports."

Penelope sorted the empty boxes from the pencils and bottles. She threw the boxes in the garbage and took her makeup upstairs to the master bathroom drawer. A box was sitting on the table.

She came downstairs, grabbed the box, and went into the living room.

"I've received the authorization from Jonathan. He does want Susan and I to talk with Jane about Cathy's whereabouts."

Liam put his phone on the coffee table and rubbed his beard.

"I think my razor should go away."

She handed him the box with the new shaver.

"The store was on my way home."

"Thank you, Penelope. Our Captain informed me of his decision via a phone call. I told him that I was against the idea. He told me you could handle Jane as you did in the expensive shop. I still disagreed."

"My job is in a detective position. Susan and I will do our job. I'm not afraid of Mrs. Beeker or her bodyguards."

Liam opened the box.

"Again, I appreciate the razor and the reminder."

Penelope knew the next few days would be stressful for both.

"Marvin is going to let go of the Malibu house. Never in a hundred years would I have seen this change coming. At least he will be familiar with the area and can keep his friends."

She also was surprised.

"Anything else happened?"

Penelope went into the kitchen and opened a bottle of wine. She poured them glasses and brought them into the living room.

"He mentioned us briefly. He said I would be a good mom."

Liam clinked her glass.

"Mr. Edmond is right for once."

Liam thought about the ship, Star Magnetic, on her northern return to Los Angeles.

The tension between them disappeared.

28 Female Detectives and Jane

Penelope drove through the tall gates of Paul and Jane Beeker's mansion.

The gates were the typical wrought iron Mediterranean affair, and the house was painted a cream stucco with a red baked brick roof. The outside shutters on the house were black, and the yard was filled with luscious plants a pink and dark rose-red color. The house was large and austere. The windows reflected the light, so it was hard to see inside. She wondered if the windows were the same in the evening.

"They probably have mechanized drapes or shades."

Penelope looked at Susan who seemed a little petrified. Petrified wouldn't go over too well with Mrs. Beeker. She would need to calm her detective friend's nerves.

"Nice house. I imagined the place would be impressive from the price of the blouses in the high-end store the woman shops. I put the four hundred fifty-dollar blouse on the pile with the others. The blouse was neatly folded again by me."

"What if she asks me a direct question? Are there any rules?"

Penelope knew Susan missed the blouse conversation.

"Answer without divulging. You know the routine we use on interviews."

"I do know, but she is smart."

"Great, we agree about her intelligence. Let's not forget, we also belong to this group plus we are skilled. We can go to the front door. I imagine the butler or bodyguard is waiting for us to arrive. I passed on brunch and opted for tea. I hope you drink the stuff. If not, take the cup and put in lots of sugar and lemon."

The front hall was ornate with mirrors and large paintings. The walls were a soft gold color as were the rugs. Two huge chandeliers gleamed as if recently polished. Penelope caught a glance at the library. The two French doors to the living room were shut. The female detectives were ushered into a garden room close to the pool. They could hear the pool water bubbling as the cleaner vents opened and shut.

"This is nice if you like bright green. Ivy wallpaper with exotic birds is different."

Penelope held her hand up to the bird's head. There were no mirrors or pictures in this room.

"The birds are life-size. It's like we are in an aviary. I shouldn't have returned the green outfit to the high-end store. The outfit would blend perfectly with this room. No, I think a white outfit would be better. Less drama."

Mrs. Beeker appeared in a lime green silk pantsuit.

"Hello, Detective Knight. I heard your comment about my green room. Perhaps I should return this pantsuit, too. I paid too much for it."

Penelope brightened.

"Hello, Mrs. Beeker. You do look better in the color than my mother. Your home is very stunning and has a nice curb appeal. The Mediterranean feel is very California."

"Call me Jane. We are past the formalities since you purchased me the water. I'm glad you approve of my designer home. Paul's father built the mansion. I'm not fond of some of the floor and wall tile. We did redo the upper floor bathrooms with quartz a year ago. Who is your friend?"

"This is Detective Clemens. She is a trainee, and I thought she might enjoy getting out for the morning instead of taking juveniles to see their shrinks."

Mrs. Beeker almost smiled. The maid brought in the tea and set the tray on a large ottoman. She poured the women each a cup. When the maid came to Detective Clemens, Susan responded. "Two sugars and three lemons."

Susan took her full porcelain cup and quickly took a sip. Her eyes grew large as the liquid was hot.

"These cups are exquisitely beautiful. The gold edging is wider than normal which says ancient. The theme of ivy repeats itself."

"The cups have been in the family for a long time. We did wallpaper this room with something more vibrant. I prefer red flowers outside and not on my walls."

Susan's hands trembled as she put the cup and saucer down for fear of breaking the gold band.

Mrs. Beeker waited until Penelope put her cup on the small table.

"Your message mentioned a discussion about my sister."

"My boss, Captain Jonathan Harrison, recommended that we pay you a social visit. He is concerned. We've been wanting to talk with her to see if she knew the four people that were killed. She seems to have disappeared."

Jane took a long sip of her tea.

"How is Jonathan? We met a long time ago when I was brash and overly confident. He probably wasn't kind in his description of me. He told me my aura was unfriendly. Of course, we argued. We agreed on bold rather than unfriendly. I'm always friendly at parties and social functions."

"He's a terrific boss, and I like his wife. Sometimes we disagree as well. Women think differently."

"You hit the target, detective."

"Getting to our visit, Detective Clemens also went to your daughter's college. She visited with some of her former instructors. They voiced their disappointment intelligent students dropped out this semester. Your daughter's name was mentioned along with some others. The detective went to her apartment to talk with her. As a former alum, she wanted to help. Cathy wasn't home. She went back recently, and your sister seems to have never returned to her apartment since the fire at the warehouse."

Jane fleetingly looked at Detective Clemens eating a lemon slice. The mention of the warehouse fire halted her movement.

"Cathy has always been a wild child. I'm older and spoiled her. She comes and goes wherever, and whenever she pleases. There is money in an account she can access at any time plus I'm sure she has some money squirreled away in a few city banks and elsewhere. Paul and I haven't seen her for some time. We talked about her last evening. Paul is quite fond of her. Neither one of us is worried."

"You don't want to submit a missing person's report?"

"No, we think that would be a disaster. She has a temper and would feel we imposed on her way of life. She's probably on some island having a private party with her strange friends. My sister orders party stuff from this island company in Mexico. If we feel there is some danger, we will call on our people to search for her."

"Do you remember any of the names of her strange friends? I'm assuming they aren't the college crowd."

"No, I didn't ask their names. They were older."

She saw a few pictures in the hallway.

"Did Cathy show you any pictures of her friends?"

Jane looked thoughtful.

"Now that you mention pictures, I did check her phone and her room once. There were no photos."

"How odd?"

Penelope knew the meeting would be considered a stalemate.

"At least you know the department is concerned. We like to help our citizens if there is something amiss."

Mrs. Beeker stood, and Susan jumped out of her chair. Penelope rose gracefully.

"Thank you for seeing us and the wonderful tea. We can find our way out."

The minute she spoke, the butler appeared.

"Landor, who is also a bodyguard, will escort you to the door. We can't have guests getting lost in our home. Sometimes there are business clients. Have a fun rest of your day, detectives."

The attendant brought around their vehicle. She was glad they used a company car. The attendant carried a gun as did the bodyguard.

Penelope drove through the gates and passed the guard station to the gated community. She noticed a car followed her until she turned to take the freeway to the office.

"The interview wasn't exactly what we hoped would happen. There seemed to be no concern regarding Cathy's absence. You did notice the guns."

Susan watched the cars on the freeway.

"She's scarier than the guns."

Penelope knew the woman was indeed scary.

"I've seen worse."

Susan had also seen worse. "I will do better next time. Any idea the cost of the teacup?"

"Probably fifteen hundred for the cup and the same for the saucer."

Susan gasped, "I almost dropped both."

Penelope knew Susan would hold her own eventually. She decided distraction always worked.

"Marvin Edmond asked about you the other day when I ran into him at the mall."

"Really? I only met the District Attorney a few times. He asked me about Carter's hand. Which mall?"

The detective told her. She glanced in her rearview mirror. There didn't appear to be anyone following them anymore. She wondered about the earlier car. There would be no reason for Jane to have the two women followed. The department knew the detectives were at the house.

She remembered their conversation in the high-end store.

Penelope tried to remember if she put the information in her revised report. She would need to recheck. Her body shivered. Penelope turned the vent, so the air would aim for the ceiling. She was suddenly cold.

Susan was reading the texts on her phone.

"Carter texted large trucks have arrived at both warehouses. Warehouse workers unloaded the trucks. The trucks have driven away, and the warehouse doors are shut. There's been no other activity for an hour."

"They probably won't move the goods until nightfall. There is a storm approaching. I imagine there will be a power outage. It won't matter."

Susan toyed with her phone.

"I went through school on a scholarship. Cathy received a free ride, and she skipped out. Unbelievable."

Penelope wasn't sure anything in life was free. Some people were granted easier access.

"We don't know what has happened to Cathy Blair. I'm sure our boss will mention the missing woman to his friends. This town is large, but hiding can be difficult for an extended period. Remember, she is beautiful and hard to miss. Plus, the connection to the

Beeker name gives her celebrity status. Some photographers might catch a glimpse of the former college student wandering the streets, restaurants, or bars. Then the beach is an attraction."

Penelope drove down the freeway some distance and slowed with the traffic.

"Did you notice how Jane Beeker avoided the four murdered people? She also didn't offer any information regarding Cathy's connection to the workers. With Cathy studying avionics and programming, there should have been knowledge shared when she went to the Beeker company."

Susan looked at the cars.

"Maybe she never visited the company."

Penelope saw an exit that would return them to the office sooner.

"In three years, I'm sure she went there at least once or twice for money," commented Penelope.

"It's interesting. I picked up that Mrs. Beeker doesn't like Cathy's strange friends, and they aren't exactly welcome in the home."

Penelope relaxed on the familiar city street. "Tension is high in the Beeker's residence is my assumption."

29 Paul and Jane Talk

Jane saw Paul's limousine in their driveway. She went looking for him in his paneled office.

"We need to talk about Cathy. Since she returned last evening, I could see that she has gotten worse."

"Jane, your sister is your problem. If you didn't ride on her case all the time, you might get along with each other. I'm surprised she walked through our door. I wouldn't have returned."

"You blame me for her bad attitude. She makes no sense. There's a brain not being used."

"I do blame you. Cathy couldn't join a protest march without you becoming unglued."

Jane couldn't believe her husband.

"My sister didn't have a clue about what she was protesting. That is the reason I didn't understand her actions. I forbid her to protest. She yelled that I was the antagonistic rich people that ruled America. Cathy had the gall to accuse us of exploiting people. We were the problem of society's current ills. I asked her what ills were encountered while living under our roof or at the nicely-decorated apartment. Richness has paved her way. She's wrong and needs to grow up."

"I'm looking for my briefcase. Have you seen the brown case? I don't care about her protesting."

Jane remembered there was a briefcase near the highbacked chair. She pointed. Paul was delighted to find the case with the shipping documents for his lawyer. He stood and knew he should say something.

His last comment was uncalled for by him. Paul felt sad inside.

"The lawyer helped her set up her business entity, and she had been creating a business plan. I'm glad she has returned. Now she can pursue her paper business. Once she gets her store going, she will calm down. My comment should be ignored. I was rude to you. We need to support her and gently stay out of her way."

Jane wasn't sure about Cathy being an entrepreneur. She accepted her husband's slip in temper. He was as tired as she was about her sister. The strain was showing. Jane secretly wished Cathy would return to Hong Kong.

"When Cathy arrived, she was limping a little bit. Have you any idea why?"

"She told me she was in an accident at the beach. Her leg got stuck in a dock board."

"Should we make her see a doctor?"

Paul buckled his brown case shut.

"I offered to take her to the emergency room or the day clinic this morning, and she refused within a second. Immediately, I dropped the idea."

Jane didn't understand why her sister wouldn't get her leg checked by a professional.

"In this heat, she wore long slacks. This isn't like her. She hasn't used our swimming pool either. Last year we couldn't keep her out of the water. I also don't like her friends. I've asked that she not bring them to our home. Cathy glared at me and shoved your bronze statue of your father's head on the floor.

Luckily, the head didn't break. My bodyguard put the sculpture on the stand again."

Paul pondered the long slacks.

"You think she is hiding her legs?"

Jane touched the highbacked chair and leaned on the top.

"I think Cathy is hiding a lot from us. Her legs might be a part of the puzzle. She's never overturned anything in the house before. Something has happened. I can't pinpoint where things went wrong. My suspicions have been aroused. Jonathan sent two female detectives to ask me about her whereabouts."

Paul looked at his wife in alarm.

"They didn't receive any information from me. I lied and told them we weren't worried about my sister's disappearance."

"The police don't know she's in our home."

"There was no reason to tell them. They want to see if she knew the four dead people. I avoided talking about the murders. Besides, Cathy told me she was going to be gone for two more weeks."

Now Paul appeared genuinely concerned.

"Good, god. She left again. I thought she might stay."

Jane was partly grateful and partly more nervous.

"She took the new clothes I purchased for her and the jacket. She also wanted cash."

Paul frowned.

"Cathy has drained her accounts already. How much did you give her?"

"I took fifteen thousand from the wall safe."

Paul looked around the room where the safe was on the wall.

"I suppose she wanted more."

Jane wondered if her husband was staying for lunch.

"We're having an excellent fish sandwich for lunch with a salad."

"I can't stay. The lawyer and I are looking over some shipping documents. I'm sorry about Cathy leaving."

Jane was disappointed.

"My idea was to give her a very minimum amount of money. This way she will need to return. I hope you can talk some sense into her when she does."

Paul picked up his briefcase.

"One more thing. The detective, Penelope, asked if I knew the names or saw any pictures of Cathy's oddball friends. I told her I didn't know nor see any. Did she tell you their names? Do you think they are dangerous?"

"There was this one person. I think she called him Steven or Stephan. I wasn't paying attention. She always hates having her picture taken. I'm not surprised by any missing friend photos. The detective was doing the standard missing person interview. I must run. Call me if you hear from Cathy again. Try to stay out of her way for her well-being and yours."

Jane watched her husband leave. His footsteps resonated in their long hallway. The front door opened and shut. The limousine drove away. Jane wanted to go away. The mansion was too large, and she was lonely. She wondered about hiring a detective to follow Cathy.

"I can do the job. My sister is my responsibility. Paul has made his feelings clear. Stay out of her way? He forgets who is in charge in this house. Cathy is not, and she never will be. She hates the rich. Isn't that a joke and a half? How many dives did I sing in before finding my husband? Lots and lots of places if my memory serves me. The sooner she returns to her apartment, the better."

Jane straightened the afghan in the room. She found a drone propeller in the fold of the couch cushions.

"How did this piece of plastic get in here?"

Jane threw the piece in the trash.

"The cleaning people aren't doing a decent job. We will fix that little problem."

She disappeared looking for her maid.

Paul stepped inside the large hallway. Jane stopped in surprise.

"I'd like to give Cathy a little more time with this new business. If your sister is a continuing problem, I will agree. We need to send her back to Hong Kong. She can finish her college degree there. The next time Cathy asks for personal money, we will not provide her the funds. We control the money for her business."

Jane was grateful. She nodded her approval. She almost told him about the plastic part. Jane let her curiosity pass.

30 Drug Enforcement

Thunder and lightning lit the night sky. Penelope was alone at the house with Dodge's dog. The dog followed her around the house. Her restlessness caused the dog to be more watchful. She rubbed her eye and viewed the dog.

"My company isn't enjoyable. I'll make us some hotdogs while we wait for the men."

She let the dog smell the hotdog package and buns. Taking the tray of meat, bread, condiments, and tools to the outdoor grill, she lit the barbeque. The dog intently kept track of each hotdog placed on the grill.

"See, I know how to cook. How hard can this be?"

After burning a few hotdogs and buns, she got the hang of the grill. The burners were turned off.

"We can eat now."

The dog immediately sat down and waited. She buttered the bun, put ketchup on, and added a cooked hotdog. She put the hotdog on a paper plate and set the plate on the deck. The dog wolfed down the tasty meat.

"You need to wait until I eat mine. You don't like mustard. I do. Here smell."

The dog shook her head.

Meanwhile, Liam waited with Dodge, Davidson, Hugh, and Carter at the first warehouse. They wanted to stay out of the main focused area and the gunfire action that would take place at the second warehouse. Hugh spoke.

"How did you figure this warehouse was a dummy set?"

Dodge explained the other ten vans weren't necessary at warehouse two.

Hugh rolled the concept through his brain.

"I think we should quietly go home after the gig at warehouse two is over and leave this other warehouse you are watching intact. People don't buy ten trucks for no reason."

"People don't buy for any reason." Liam was thinking the same thing. Dodge figured out the logic.

"Manning meets Lourdes. Lourdes knows Merk. These trucks at warehouse one wasn't a foil at all. They will be used later for a different shipment by different people. All Lourdes did was buy trucks for someone and pay Manning for the lease. Merk is our guess, but there could be someone else involved."

"I'll talk to Drug Enforcement to stand down on this warehouse."

Carter quipped, "Will they follow your direction?"

Liam got a strange look on his face.

"They will, or they can get busted by Jonathan's wrath on their superior officer."

Hugh was rolling his wedding ring around. Liam noticed.

"What are you thinking?"

Hugh looked at his ring.

"Why would Merk put his nose across the line? In the past, he walked on top but never went over."

Davidson shrugged.

"Money!"

"He has money. His house is in the hill neighborhood for crying out loud," said Hugh excitedly.

"Dodge, you've known Merk longer than anyone, what's your conclusion?"

"Hugh has brought up a good point. We might want to park our theory. Maybe the compass isn't pointing true north."

Liam waved his hand for silence. He put his phone on speaker and turned the volume lower. They could hear shouting, gunfire, and squealing of tires. After twenty minutes, one of the drug enforcement people talked with Liam.

"We've arrested Manning and Lourdes for illegal drug possession. The dockworkers and truck drivers are going to jail. The warehouse is on lockdown. The mission was successful. Warehouse one wasn't touched, and my men have pulled back per your request."

Liam thanked the officer. He disconnected the call. Liam called his boss and told him the news and their theory about warehouse one. They thought Lourdes could provide more on the company who ordered stuff for warehouse one, but they shouldn't approach him yet. They didn't want to scare the people off. Lourdes should be heavily guarded.

"Carter, Hugh, and I will leave. This next weekend, the two detectives will give Dodge and Davidson a break. Congratulations, everyone!"

Dodge approached Liam.

"I'll get my dog after breakfast tomorrow. Penelope told me she bought bacon and sausage. Save me a platter with eggs."

"I sure will."

Liam and the two detectives went back to the office.

Carter stopped Liam.

"Should I be worried about Susan?"

Liam hadn't heard any problems with the detective.

"Penelope told me she was doing fine. The interview with Jane Beeker went well. Hugh felt the same about her skills on the job. Are you having some reservations?"

"No, forget I said anything. She's doing fine at work. I was thinking from a personal perspective."

"Good to know. I have no clue how she feels about you on a personal level. Romance has not always been my forte. It took me years to find Penelope. Even then, she was hard to convince. Oh, women aren't always truthful."

"Gee, thanks a lot, Liam. Hugh told me the same thing."

"See you next week. One more thing. You and Hugh are getting new wooden desks next week. Penelope made me order the more expensive chairs."

Carter stood with his mouth open. Then he jumped for joy. He emptied the drawer that always broke and threw the detested object in the trash.

31 Dinner at the Knight's Beach House

Penelope, Emma, and Susan watched the men try to put a table together and some lounge chairs for the party at Liam's beach house. The beer and sodas were in large plastic tubs filled with ice. The patio tiles were brand new, and the backyard area was looking much more like a livable outdoor space. The furniture would complete the new look.

Liam kissed his wife.

"They have five minutes to finish assembling the furniture, or else they are fired."

Hugh was in close range.

"I heard that."

"I'm glad you installed the privacy screen. Our neighbor is officially blocked from our view."

Emma handed her husband a beer. Dodge and Carter set the table upright, and the lounge chairs received their soft cushions. There were two double lounge chairs and four chairs around the table. Hugh and Emma sat together. Hugh bounced up and down.

"Nice cushions."

Liam grabbed the steaks.

"Put the foil potatoes in the warming oven. I see the salad and bun bread is ready."

Penelope did as she was told and turned the burner to warm.

"Hugh, those cushions cost me a fortune."

He watched as the detective put his feet on the ottoman.

Liam groaned.

"Too bad Davidson and his wife couldn't make the party."

"Guys, I need help with the steaks."

Dodge's dog jumped around joyfully as he threw the frisbee. As soon as Liam carried the steaks outside, the dog lost focus.

The group sat around with their wicker plates and paper plates on top eating dinner. There was quiet for a few moments.

"These steaks are great, Liam. Which meat market did you go to this time?"

"Emma helped me by picking them up from your favorite butcher."

"I thought they tasted familiar," commented Hugh.

Everyone made quick work of the food. Emma brought out the cream cheese brownies with caramel sauce and a chew bone for the dog. In the kitchen, the women cleaned up the dishes and leftovers. They went back outside to join the men.

"The reason for the dinner wasn't only free food."

The men grumbled. Liam understood.

"Penelope and Susan went to interview Jane Beeker. I understand she was polite."

The men clapped.

"However, on the way out of the housing complex, a car followed them to the freeway. I checked with all our organizations, and we currently aren't watching Paul's mansion. Per Penelope, there was no front license plate, and she couldn't tell who was driving. The car was a standard black model name brand car which is typical for this area in the neighborhood. The make and model would be hard to find without a plate number."

"Mrs. Beeker wouldn't hire a car to follow someone so close to her home," said Hugh.

Dodge threw the ball for his dog.

"Are we thinking about some organization?"

Liam wasn't sure.

"I don't think the Beeker's are connected to any mob. We do have a problem with the fact that someone may be following the Beeker's. Jane mentioned that she thought I was following her when we went fishing, and she met Penelope at the high-end store."

"Where should we go from here? Are you wanting us to find out who's following the Beeker's? Shouldn't that fall on their people?" asked Carter.

Dodge stood and threw the ball again. He grabbed a second beer.

"I believe Liam wants us to be careful and pay attention. Because the entity is unknown, we don't know their agenda. In other words, who is watching whom and why? There may be more nut jobs in the area than we realize."

"Good analysis, Dodge. We have put out some feelers with the police that patrol the Beeker area and have alerted our organization. For now, that is the best we can do."

Liam grabbed a soda out of the tub. He would need to drive Dodge and the dog home.

Hugh stood and Emma told everyone, "I appreciated getting out of my house this evening. The kids also needed a break from mom. Goodnight."

"Goodnight," chimed in the others. Penelope walked them to the front door. Hugh turned.

"Was she polite?"

"Jane was cautiously careful and protected by a bodyguard. There seemed to be an abundance of firepower at the house."

"I'll bet."

Penelope went back to her guests. Carter and Susan left. Dodge, the dog, and Liam got ready to leave.

"You sure you don't want to ride along?"

"I'll be fine. Get our friend home."

"Lock the doors. You know where the guns are hidden. Maybe I should hire you a bodyguard."

"Go."

Liam kissed his wife, "Nice party. The furniture works."

Penelope looked at her kitchen and checked outside. The men took care of the boxes, plastic, and paper. The plastic tubs were empty, and the remaining beer and soda were on the deck. She grabbed the beer and put the bottles in the refrigerator. Next, the soda was put away. She locked the doors.

Penelope checked the drawer with the gun to make sure it was there. She put the clip in the compact nine-millimeter gun. Then she made sure the safety was on.

"At least I feel a little better."

She knew the case was putting everyone on edge. Catching Lourdes and Manning was a minor part of this case. Their days were numbered the minute Lourdes stepped out of the prison gates. The shipment of drugs could have come from anywhere.

"We are getting a new detective this week. She will work with Carter and Susan. The extra person will help."

Penelope reread the note. The person was a transfer from San Diego. Her name was Barbara Branden. She was about Hugh's age. The reason for her transfer was medical for her ill husband. His treatments were in LA.

"Susan could train her. This would free up Carter to work the warehouse and Dodge to do other things. I wonder if that's the plan. Either way, I need to shoot something soon."

32 Shooting Range

Liam saw Penelope's text. He quickly responded.

Penelope took her gun belt off and found her shooting gloves and goggles. Liam's sports car pulled next to hers.

"Hey, stranger, fancy meeting you with a gun at my favorite hunting grounds. Let's go shoot some buffalo."

"You do know a full-size buffalo costs around six thousand dollars apiece."

"No kidding!"

Liam took his gun belt off, opened his trunk for his goggles and gloves.

"I think we both needed to get rid of some frustration that we are feeling."

"The gun in the drawer in the kitchen has the clip inside. I was nervous after our guests left."

Liam steered Penelope inside. They registered and were shown their booths. After a half-hour of shooting, they both quit.

"Feel better now?"

"I feel immensely relieved. At least I still know how to shoot a weapon with my husband around."

"Pressure. You do shoot better in a situation that is not ideal."

"Thanks."

Liam walked with her outside. He nodded to several policemen he knew.

"Penelope, we need to talk about protection."

She leaned against her car.

"Go ahead."

Liam watched as a few cars left the shooting range.

"I think you need a bodyguard. Two guns are better than one. This strange car that followed you from the Beeker's is the reason."

Penelope looked at her husband. She didn't want to be coddled by her boss.

"I'm fine."

She moved to get in her vehicle.

"Listen to me."

Penelope didn't want to listen.

"I'm worried. We have someone who followed you specifically. They didn't follow me or Hugh or Susan. They didn't even follow Carter."

"You can get a bullet just like me. Why don't we hire the bodyguard for you?"

Liam looked at the dust appearing on his car from the gravel parking lot.

"They need to fix this place with mountains of cement. We go back to the office and talk some more."

"Okay."

The two detectives reached the office. Liam was called into Jonathan's office, and Penelope was free to talk with Hugh and Carter.

"Nice desks. The chairs are perfect. Let me sit in one."

Hugh jumped up, and Penelope slowly slid into the seat.

"Any idea why Liam is in our boss's office?"

Hugh sat on his new desk.

"Both of us know. I'll tell the story."

"There's a story."

Carter opened his congratulatory basket of fruit that was on his desk. Penelope took an apple.

"Nice of the boss to make a production about the desks. Getting to the story, the Star Majestic is on her journey northward. The Captain is showing the information to our leader. Our understanding is the tequila has been loaded. We think they are planning when, and who will raid the small warehouse in Long Beach."

Penelope was delighted.

"The drone parts might be in the straw in the expensive tequila crates."

"I don't know exactly if that is what they are thinking," responded Hugh.

"Where else could the parts be located?"

Carter interjected.

"We're thinking about other theories. However, Paul Beeker has decided this is an express shipment which means things will go through customs faster."

"His clients will bail if they don't get their expensive tequila bottles."

Hugh nodded.

"There is more."

Penelope crunched on her apple.

"I have no clue."

"Jane called Jonathan today to let him know Cathy has shown up at their home."

Penelope couldn't believe Cathy was alive.

"Mrs. Beeker called Jonathan and not me."

Hugh took an apple.

"You aren't exactly friends with the woman."

Susan arrived, and they informed her of the new happenings with the case.

"Did anyone see this Cathy person besides Mrs. Beeker?"

Penelope nodded. She also wanted to know.

"Paul confirmed the long-lost daughter of his wife did return. He complained about the noise from her room. Cathy has been taking flying lessons and watching flying videos. She handed him the bill and left."

Susan sat down and grabbed a banana. The four detectives disbursed when Liam came out of his boss's office. He went into his office and slammed the door. Penelope waited ten minutes and knocked.

"Come in."

Penelope handed him an orange. He began peeling the outside. Breaking the orange slices off, she let him eat a few.

"I heard. At least the ship is on its way. Any idea of how we approach the warehouse?"

"The Captain will let me know."

Penelope sat in a chair and wondered why the sudden change.

"Paul Beeker has complained about our department."

"What?"

"He found out about your interview with Jane, and we are forbidden to enter his properties. He has told our Captain that he will sue our department if we trespass again."

Penelope sat back in the chair completely dumbfounded.

"Trespass. Are you serious? The butler or bodyguard opened the door. We entered."

"I know what happened. I read your report. Jonathan will get with our attorney. We are on hold for the moment."

Penelope felt helpless.

"The new desks look perfect. I sat in the chair."

Liam halfway smiled.

"The fruit tasted fresh. I enjoyed shooting with you today. We haven't gone shooting together for a long time. You beat me, but not by much."

Penelope was glad Liam was back to his normal self again.

"I wonder why Cathy took flying lessons. Did they say where she took lessons? You can't learn via videos. We could ask Dodge to check on her."

"She would probably take them locally. I'll get him to call around. There are all kinds of ways to learn to fly and to move illegal goods."

Penelope left his office. She was going to interview Cathy's college friends. Susan might have missed something.

Using her computer, she found the names and phone numbers and printed the page. Next, she reviewed Simon's autopsy report.

"There aren't any dental records completed. How did we know the body belonged to the man named Simon Needham?"

She shuffled some papers.

"The parents notified the police their son didn't call them for over a year, nor did they see him. They read in the newspaper about potential victims from the company he worked for and the missing identification papers. When they tried to call his phone after receiving a recent text, the number was disconnected. The parents viewed the body and confirmed to the coroner the person looked like their son. The height, body weight, and hair appeared the same."

She undid her hair tie.

"Not exactly rocket science. But still? The parents are upset when they visit the morgue. The person might be their son. Might be isn't good enough in my opinion."

She shut down her computer. Penelope drove to the beach house. Liam showed up with takeout.

33 Discovery

Penelope was done with her interviews with the college students. She did find out that Cathy dated someone outside of the college crowd. No one ever met the man. She only knew the person who worked for the Beeker Company in some capacity. They also told her that Cathy owned a pilot's license. She wondered what type of lessons Cathy took recently.

She stopped at the high-end clothing shop and talked with the salesperson who helped her in the past.

"Did Jane Beeker ever bring her sister with her shopping in your store?"

The saleswoman put another woman's outfit in a shopping bag.

"Here you go, Mrs. Drann."

She motioned for Penelope to follow her into the employee lounge.

"I met Cathy only once, and that was enough for me. Whenever I saw her enter the shop, I disappeared on my break."

"Please explain."

"Mrs. Beeker ordered six dresses for some fancy function she was having. She brought Cathy into the shop. Unfortunately, we received a shipment of leather jackets and boots that Cathy locked onto instead of the dresses. There was a terrible fight between the two women. Mrs. Beeker, naturally, backed down."

"You are telling me Cathy is headstrong."

"I would say she is unnaturally way out of control. Normally, I'm used to our client's family persons, big, tall, or short, but she was a monster and takes the cake."

Penelope was getting the picture. She drove to the office. Liam waved her into his office. The rest of the office bullpen area was empty.

"Cathy took helicopter classes per Dodge. He knows the instructor, and the airfield she practiced. There was a young man with her once. He drove a junk car. We've sent the image to our people. They have sent us their information."

Liam showed her the blurred image.

"I don't understand the lines on the image."

He grinned.

"The lines represent the same facial dimensions of a dead person. The parents gave us a photograph finally."

Penelope knew who the man was with Cathy.

"Simon isn't dead. The dead person was someone else. This someone else was disposable. We aren't going to notify Simon's parents until after the case."

Liam backed away from his desk. Penelope explained, "I had a hunch."

"When did you have this hunch?"

Penelope knew Liam was getting defensive. She shouldn't have said the man's name.

"Yesterday. I reread the coroner's report. I thought my idea was crazy. If the man was alive, he did have something to do with the other's deaths. The thought was inconceivable."

Liam watched his wife.

"You learned in detective class the inconceivable happens. Did you forget?"

"No." Penelope sighed. She informed him of what the college students and the salesperson told her about Cathy.

"Your reaction to the information?"

"I think Jane has tried to protect her daughter. Paul may have ignored impending signs. The daughter may be running with Simon. Their objective and how many people know about their plan might be limited. I think we are talking about a small group."

Liam frowned.

"Let me explain. Limited in that they have this group of people, but only one or two are calling the shots. The rest follow like sheep."

"My approach is a little different. I think Jane is someway involved. I'm not sure about Paul. Simon is dangerous and could be important. He was or is interested in avionics. Let's say he's obsessed. Cathy might be naïve although she's well-educated. She could be rolling along with Simon."

"Naïve could get you killed," said Penelope.

Liam backed away from his wife.

"Wow. I struck a nerve."

"You are the one who asked for my reaction."

Liam saw his phone buzz. "Our Captain has given us the approval to proceed with the pursuit of the Star Magnetics' potential import improprieties once they reach land. The team has been advised. That's all."

Penelope knew she was being dismissed. She went to her desk. Susan introduced her to the new person.

"Hello, Detective Branden, welcome aboard."

The elderly woman extended her hand, "Call me Barbara. We came from the shooting range, and my desk is in the corner. I'm happy to be here."

Susan grabbed Barbara's hand.

"We need to meet Kamilla. She does the day assignments when we aren't on a case."

Penelope shot Susan a look of appreciation. She needed a minute or five.

Dodge stopped by her desk.

"Hi, beautiful lady. Liam's busy and you aren't."

"Dodge, I'm glad you stopped by today. I needed a cheerful face."

He understood.

"Liam is strained lately. The pressure always increases toward the end. We're getting close."

"I know."

Dodge looked at Penelope.

"I'm glad one of us is going to be level-headed in this fight. My body is going to be on your side all the way. You have this aura. I'm following you."

Penelope couldn't believe Dodge was flirting. Liam stood behind Dodge.

"Well, Liam, there you are. I was talking with a beautiful woman, but I'm ready for our meeting."

Dodge turned to Penelope.

"We'll talk some more as soon as I get rid of your husband."

Penelope watched the two men walk away. "Dodge was Dodge."

She saw the back of Marvin's head in Jonathan's office. Penelope grabbed her bag and left the office.

Walking down the street, she heard a car approaching. Penelope glanced over her shoulders and made an automatic leap into some bushes. The car drove on the sidewalk where she was previously walking and sped off.

Several shop owners came out of their shops to help her. A policeman helped her stand.

"Did you get a license plate number?"

Penelope didn't. No one did because there was none. The policeman took her information and called the accident in. He walked Penelope back to the office and put her bag on her desk.

"You should have the leg checked out.

"I'm fine. Thank you for helping me to reach my desk."

Penelope was shaken. She went to the restroom to wash the cuts on her right leg. The other leg contained minor scratches. Undoing the cloth bandage strips, she put some salve on the cuts and covered the wounds. Next, she noticed her arm was bleeding. She grabbed a paper towel and slapped the towel on her arm. Opening the aspirin bottle, Susan came into the restroom and saw Penelope.

"Oh, my gosh, you are hurt."

"Remember the car with no license plate."

Susan did remember.

"Does Liam know?"

"Can you get me a glass of water?"

"Sure."

Susan disappeared and came back with a glass spilling over. Penelope drank the water.

"One more favor. My arm could use a bandage."

Susan cleaned the wound and carefully put the bandage on.

"What else?"

"I need a ride home."

Once they were in the car, Penelope sent Liam a text to let him know she would be at home.

"Please don't say anything. I'm trying to figure out how to explain what happened. Liam goes overboard."

Susan helped her inside and change her clothes. Once Penelope was settled in a chair, she waited until the delivery boy brought the food.

"I appreciate your helping me very much."

"I could stay."

Penelope needed Susan gone. Susan understood.

"Take care."

Susan left and fifteen minutes later Liam came home. He saw the food bags and dished them a plate of food. He handed Penelope her plate.

"Are you cold? You are covered with the blanket."

Penelope pushed the blanket off.

"I'm no longer cold."

She pushed the chicken around her plate. He noticed she wasn't eating her Kung Pau. Tears developed in her eyes. Liam put his plate and hers aside.

"I'm sorry," said Liam.

Penelope knew she needed to tell him.

"This isn't about Cathy. The car without the license plate tried to run me over. I have a few scratches, but I was very scared."

Liam looked at her leg. She showed him her arm.

"Oh, baby, come here."

He let her cry. She tried to tell him between sobs.

"You should get the police report tomorrow. I didn't even think to grab my gun."

Liam shook his head at the miserable person who tried to wipe out his wife.

"At least you jumped away from the curb and sidewalk. I'm pulling Dodge into the office to protect you next week."

Penelope didn't object.

Liam helped her up and put her in his sports car. He brought her some apple juice.

"I'll be right back as soon as I put our food in a cooler and pack your makeup. We're going to stay at the condominium."

"Bring a nightie and some underwear."

Liam stuffed some of Penelope's things and his items in a suitcase. He put the suitcase and cooler in the trunk and drove to their condo. He helped his wife into the elevator with their bags and settled her in the master bedroom.

"I am glad we came and are taking time off."

"We needed to get away."

Liam tucked her in and kissed her.

"I have to make some calls. I will be back to snuggle."

He called Jonathan and Dodge. He and Penelope were taking a long weekend and wouldn't be in the office until Tuesday morning. The others on the team were informed.

34 Extended Weekend

Liam showered and crawled into bed. Penelope moved closer. He laid awake for a long time thinking. She raised.

"Go back to sleep. We're safe."

"We've reached our condominium."

"Yes."

He could feel her disappear into a deep sleep. Liam slept fitfully until morning. He kept seeing a black car with darkened windows.

He awoke with a jolt and checked on Penelope. Her eyes flashed awake.

"Let's get you to the bathroom, and I can make us breakfast next."

"I need a shower."

"I'll help."

He held out his hand. Penelope stood, and he held her close for a long time.

"We forgot eggs."

"I remembered to pack the eggs in the cooler but forgot the bread."

"There's a loaf in the freezer with some butter," said Penelope.

"You are feeling better?"

"Much better."

Liam started the shower for her and put her shampoo and towel within reach.

"I'll start breakfast. Don't be too long."

There was a knock at the door. Liam took the scrambled eggs off the stove and opened the door. He held out his hand for the extra change. Both men carried the packages and set them on the counter.

"Thanks, guys, I appreciate your help."

Penelope came around the corner in her bathrobe.

"Security went shopping for us."

He handed Penelope her plate of eggs and toast. They ate quickly and put the groceries away. Liam put their dishes in the dishwasher.

"What plans do we have today?"

"No surfing. I'm worried about your cuts."

"You look tired."

Liam was exhausted.

"We can go back to sleep, but I need some help changing my bandages."

"Haven't we been here before?"

She remembered and liked her husband taking care of her. They went into the bathroom and put ointment and dry gauze on her legs. Liam carried her to bed. She pulled him down beside her.

Liam kissed his wife, and she kissed him back. He heard his phone ringing as did Penelope.

"I think we have half an hour."

Penelope pulled him closer. The two lovers connected.

Liam watched as Penelope fell asleep again. He checked his phone messages and set the timer for two hours. Liam crawled under the covers and dozed off.

When he awoke, Penelope was missing. He ran into the living room and saw her on the patio. He relaxed and dressed. Liam joined her.

"I'm finally rested."

She moved her feet, and he sat on the end of the chaise lounge.

Liam laid his head on her chest.

"We should do this more often. Do you want to talk about yesterday?"

"No."

"Do you want to discuss work?"

"No."

"We could talk about this weekend, and how I want to be held for hours on end."

She wrapped her arms around her husband. It was all Liam needed.

The rest of their weekend was pretty much the same. On occasion, they went for a jog or lulled around the pool. Liam showed her some simple recipes to cook.

They made popcorn and tried the fudge. Penelope forgot to stir the pot. They gave up on fudge.

The young couple did talk about what they wanted next and their future. The time together was necessary for cementing their relationship. They agreed professional opinions stayed at the office. There would be disagreements on cases just like before they were married.

Monday, they drove to Los Angeles.

"Are you going to be ready for the office," asked Liam.

"I think I'll be ready."

"If any problems, you will tell me?"

He pulled into the beach house driveway, and Liam punched the door opener. The garage door lifted

"I will."

"Good."

Liam parked and made sure the garage door closed. He followed his wife inside.

"Come here for a minute."

Penelope stepped into his arms.

"Did I tell you how gorgeous you look in the moonlight?"

"Only ten times."

"You look gorgeous one more time."

"Flattery this late in the evening is dangerous."

"I hope so."

Liam kissed her passionately. Penelope felt they were back together again. They were where they started.

"I love you."

"We love each other."

She took his hand, and they raced to their bedroom. There was no need to turn the light on. Their touch was familiar even in the dark.

35 One Shipment from Star Magnetic

The police waited with Liam and Hugh for the large truck to arrive. The workers unloaded the truck at the Beeker's Long Beach warehouse. Penelope and Barbara waited in a car a short distance away as did Carter and Susan. They were on the outskirts of the warehouse in case anything went wrong.

Once the truck left, two small white vans appeared from warehouse one. The police figured the vans might eventually transport the drone parts.

"Shouldn't there be more vans?" asked Barbara.

"I'm not sure."

Penelope checked her radio. The radio was silent. They waited for thirty minutes. She began to tap her feet nervously.

"Shouldn't we call them?"

Penelope wanted to call the lead detective.

"We are to remain silent."

After an hour, Carter's vehicle pulled alongside. Susan rolled her window open.

"Have you heard anything?"

Penelope looked at her cell phone.

"Nothing as of yet."

"Carter and I will take the external road, circle the block, and see what is happening."

After ten minutes, they drove to where Penelope and Barbara waited. Carter parked, and the two detectives joined them.

"There's a large limousine at the warehouse. We saw Paul Beeker and his lawyer arguing with the police and Liam. The scene did not look good. Beeker brought another vehicle of his bodyguards. Guns have been drawn by the police. They aren't letting them into the warehouse until all the cases and boxes are unpacked."

The four waited for another two hours.

"We should drive by again."

The radio finally came on. The voice was Liam's.

"Move out and return to the office for a meeting."

Penelope was going to ask Liam a question when he abruptly disconnected the call.

"We have our orders. Come on Barbara."

They watched the two detectives leave the area. Barbara looked out the windshield.

"We should at least do a drive-by to satisfy our curiosity."

Penelope wanted to stop at the warehouse.

"We will follow orders. There is a reason Liam does not want us to be seen by Mr. Beeker, his lawyer, and the bodyguards."

Barbara understood the orders were given, and they needed to follow them. The two women returned to the office. She noticed their Captain was talking with the department's attorney and the Chief.

"There's trouble brewing. Let's make a batch of coffee at my desk. I'll get Carter to make coffee at Liam's desk. I think we are going to need a heavy dose of caffeine."

Carter went into Liam's desk and got the coffee going. He came to Penelope's desk. She handed everyone a cup of coffee. They saw Liam and Hugh go into the Captain's office. The door was shut. She saw none of the men were drinking coffee.

"Come on Susan, give me a hand with some trays. Jonathan's secretary is out for the day per Kamilla."

They fixed five cups of coffee with the cream, sugar packets, and stirrers. Penelope lightly tapped on Jonathan's door.

"Come in."

Penelope carried the hot coffee cups. She went to Jonathan and the chief first. After distributing the coffee and leaving the condiment tray, the women left. Penelope gently closed the door. They sat around Penelope's desk drinking their coffee.

None of the detectives knew what transpired, but they could guess.

After an hour, the meeting was disbursed. Hugh came over.

"There's a fifteen-minute break, and we meet in Liam's office. Carter and I will get us some scones or bagels. Dodge and Davidson will be here shortly."

"Take Barbara with you. Susan and I will make more coffee and find some cups."

The two women went into the break room holding the bakery bags. The rolls were put on trays. They watched Carter finish making more coffee and put the filled cups on trays in Liam's office. The women brought the rolls.

A frazzled Liam and Hugh stood by Liam's desk. Liam clicked on the projector. The map of the containers on the ship appeared.

"The tequila cases and boxes did not contain any drone parts. Our boys were careful with the bottles. Nothing was broken except ten of the expensive wood crates. They didn't open them correctly. Unfortunately, Mr. Beeker and his lawyer arrived. We explained our reasons for being there and showed him the search warrant. They promised to sue our department. We promised to pay for the damaged boxes."

Liam turned to the ship map.

"We still believe there may be a container on the Star Magnetic that holds the drone parts. Of course, we did not tell nor show Mr. Beeker our second warrant which gives us the right to search any of his properties or shipments."

Hugh handed a copy of the ship's manifest to everyone.

"I want you to study the map and get together in the large conference room. I've reserved the room all day. Think about the possibilities where drone parts might be stored. Grab a roll and get to work."

Liam turned off his projector. The other detectives did as they were told. Penelope waited until everyone left the room. Hugh took one of the trays of rolls.

"Thank you for the coffee. The refreshments helped diffuse the disappointment."

"I looked at your container ship while it was on the wall."

Liam grabbed a raisin scone and leaned on his desk.

"At least someone was paying attention."

Penelope frowned.

"Come here. I'm in a bad mood. I need a hug."

She stepped in front of him. He put his arms around her.

"This scene was bad. I thought I was going to get punched in the face by Paul. I was ready to deck him for some of the names he called me. Then he started calling me names in Spanish. The police objected to those names. The bodyguards withdrew their guns. I thought I was in a war zone."

Penelope pushed his hair from his brow.

"We should stop doing this hugging. Our boss probably isn't appreciative."

Liam let her go. Jonathan stuck his head in the door and took a scone.

"The coffee was great, Penelope. Raisin scones are my favorite. Carry on."

Jonathan left.

"You were talking about the ship image. Any ideas regarding the containers?"

"Yes. The container will be at the top level."

Liam smiled.

"I think we already figured that one out."

"When Susan and I interviewed Jane Beeker about Cathy, she said something odd."

Liam could count on his wife to notice the odd.

"Go ahead. Anything unusual will be examined."

"I need to remember. Give me a second."

Liam watched her. He knew her recall of conversations was excellent.

Regarding Cathy's disappearance, Jane dismissed the idea. Her comment was, "She's probably on some island having a private party. My sister orders party stuff from this island company in Mexico."

Liam's face was motionless.

"Well, what do you think?"

He went to his computer and opened a file.

"Did she give you the name of the firm?"

Penelope's eyes sparkled. She pointed to a name on the manifest paper he gave the detectives.

"Isla Santos Paper Products?"

She nodded.

"I know the odds of there being drones in the boxes might be slim, but sometimes a stronger arrow hits the mark."

"Why don't you brainstorm with the others, and we'll see what they have for theories? Please ask Dodge and Hugh to come to my office. Dodge and Hugh have some friends in Mexico. We'll make some calls."

36 Pizza Office Meeting

Liam ordered twelve boxes of pizza and large cartons of cold sodas for lunch. Davidson's wife brought two huge plastic bowls of a fruit and berry mix with plastic bowls, paper plates, and forks. The team ate lunch in the conference room. Jonathan joined them for lunch.

Their various ideas were written all over the whiteboards. The boss was impressed with the ideas. He stopped at Penelope's half board. There were three stars on her board.

"Liam, I'm going to leave you in charge of your meeting. The ideas are exceptionally good. The pizza and fruit were very filling."

"Thank you, sir. We're going to decide our next approach with my guidance, of course."

Jonathan left.

"Okay, everyone, we start our meeting in twenty minutes. Come back and get comfortable. Move the chairs and tables around if you like. I'm going to get my computer and notes."

The men put the empty pizza boxes in the garbage. The girls moved all the remaining pizza into two boxes and put them in the refrigerator. They left the fruit out and combined the bowls. The men moved the tables aside and put the chairs in a half-circle near the whiteboards.

Everyone took a break. They came back and assembled in the chairs. Liam returned.

"We start. All of us agree Container 10 is a higher probability rather than Container 11 which contains fabric. The inside of the rolls might be too small for the body of the drone. Container 12 is low refrigeration with pork rinds and dried meat products. The pork is too transparent and large. The dried meat packages are too small. The cases are a plastic see-through design. A person could easily see a drone's body. Container 13 has cheese products that come in round plastic containers. Again, the size was too small. The thought was there could be layers of drones in between. The time to load the product this way would be too long. We ruled out the grain containers and any container carrying fruit or liquids."

He looked at his audience.

"Container 10 will be our focus. We checked the dock where the container was unloaded with a police helicopter. She is still there. Dodge and Hugh, your turn."

Liam joined his wife. He squeezed her hand. Hugh spoke first.

"We contacted some friends of ours and the firm, Isla Santos Paper Products, ships to the States, Mexico, and Brazil. The company has a huge manufacturing plant where they make the party supplies. I'm sure all of you have purchased their Hawaiian-looking grass skirts, coconut decorations, and pirate masks for your last party."

The crowd laughed.

"There also is a separate shipping plant which might be where the drones were inserted into special boxes. The night shift loads the specialty orders where the day shift uses automation. We believe the drones are in a specialty order."

Hugh sat down. Dodge stood.

"The belief is that once the Container 10 is unloaded, they won't select the warehouse in Long Beach. They don't want to risk another raid by the police. Our perps will look for another warehouse. Warehouse number one was probably created as a backup plan for real paper products. We're hoping we are correct. Therefore, Davidson and I will continue our watch."

Dodge took a drink of his soda. There was something that bothered him. He erased his idea and drew a map of warehouse one on the whiteboard space.

"There's also the open field near the warehouse one about three blocks away. The perps might use a helicopter to escape if they need to flee. I've dropped my bird in the open field once or twice. Or the roads as you can see quickly lead to major freeways from this exact spot."

Dodge pointed at Liam. The lead detective took the floor.

"We have some idea of suspects. The Beeker's haven't been ruled out of the equation nor their lawyer. Because the goods might have shipped on their company's vessel, they could be liable. They could be heavily involved or not. We also have a family member named Cathy Blair. The possibility also exists a Simon Needham may still be alive. Any other suspects could be their friends and associates. Are they dangerous? The answer is an absolute yes. Someone has a game going. A lot of money can be made in the illegal drone business. Swarm drones are the new thing thieves are marketing."

Liam coughed. Penelope handed him a soda. He opened the container and took a sip.

"Any questions?"

Carter asked, "Do we have a picture of Simon other than his work photo?"

"I have our people drawing potential changes he might attempt to make to disguise himself. Those will come across once I approve of them."

Liam saw no further questions.

"Good. Here's the plan. Once we have the photos of Simon and Cathy, I want the extra detectives hitting the streets. Create your maps. We're specifically looking for information on where these two individuals may be living. Don't rock the boat too much and don't approach. We don't want them to go underground."

Penelope knew the plan. She raised her hand.

"Penelope."

"Once the large truck moves from the warehouse, we will be notified?"

"Yes. The police will track the truck. Once the boxes are unloaded, we will wait to see who appears for collection. Our theory is the shipment will be the drone parts. We believe the cameras and controllers may come from somewhere else. We're debating whether this warehouse will be used or not for putting the drones together. On that point, we have various opinions."

Liam was done. His team knew what he knew for the moment. The ground beneath them was a minefield. They could be stepping into another mess.

He remembered a movie about gangsters caught on a dirt road. The bullet holes were many.

"The work is waiting detectives. Be careful. Make sure your guns are loaded, and you have extra clips. We stay in groups of two for safety reasons. You are dismissed."

The others left the room. Dodge grabbed a box of pizza. Hugh put the other box and fruit on his desk. Penelope waited to talk with Liam.

"The meeting went well."

"This next job is going to be dangerous. Be prepared for gunfire."

"You think they will resort to weapons and murder?"

"They have already murdered seven people."

Liam took his notes and computer.

"You and Barbara can erase the whiteboards."

Barbara stepped into the conference room. Penelope handed her a clean erasure.

"The others sneaked out. We get dirty work."

Barbara began wiping the board.

37 Warehouse One Movement

Dodge and Davidson were notified the large truck was being loaded from Container 10.

"Nuts, I parked my helicopter in the field. I was going to race in and out today. I dropped my dog off with my vet at the airfield this morning. He ate something outside that made him ill."

They received a note from Liam to get ready. The two detectives watched as the large truck backed up to warehouse one. The workers unloaded the boxes and drove off.

Dodge received a text from his vet. He became agitated. Davidson asked him what was wrong.

"Someone put out rat poison outside to eliminate my dog. We need to get those people."

They waited until two in the morning. There was no movement.

"Are the others still in place?"

Dodge looked at his watch.

"The police are still around, I think."

Dodge saw a pricey black car pull in. The woman who stepped out was Jane Beeker. There was no one with her.

"This is certainly a surprise."

A few minutes later, Paul Beeker arrived in his car without a bodyguard and went inside the warehouse.

"Two people have made a party entrance."

Dodge talked with Liam. Neither of them had any idea why the husband and wife were inside minus their bodyguards at this time of the night.

"You stay near the back and tell Davidson to go around to the front door. Don't move once in place. The police officer and I are going inside."

Dodge heard five shots fired in rapid succession. He ran inside the warehouse with his gun hand extended. Someone fired at him and hit his right hand. Dodge dropped his gun and fell to the floor. He heard running feet and the front door slam.

There was another shot. Dodge grabbed his gun. The policeman was dead. Jane Beeker was bleeding, and Paul Beeker lay on the floor. He saw Liam with a leg wound close to Paul. A box of parts was on the floor.

Dodge saw the cameras inside the warehouse were turned off. Penelope appeared in the doorway out of breath. She assessed the situation and went to Mrs. Beeker first. The woman appeared to be wounded the worst. She shouted.

"Liam?"

"I'm all right. Dodge, you go after them."

He radioed Hugh.

"Where the heck are the backup policemen? Get me ambulances now!"

She heard Liam shout the address. Penelope leaned down. Jane tried to speak.

"I followed my sister. Her car is out front. There's a side door. She must have used it. I knew she was to blame. Cathy asked me to arrange the tour. I somehow helped her kill those people. I couldn't tell

Paul. She aimed at me tonight and shot your husband instead. Her boyfriend shot me. He aimed for my heart. His eyes were filled with loathing."

"Be still. Liam has called for ambulances."

"I'm not going to be around."

Penelope was upset. Jane shouldn't have to die.

"Be strong. Medical vehicles are on their way."

The woman coughed.

"Tell Paul that I'm sorry. I didn't know until now how bad she was."

Penelope saw the blood on the floor, and Jane closed her eyes. She was gone. The detective heard more shots outside. She ran to Liam.

"Give me your scarf."

He tied the scarf around his leg.

"Jane is gone."

"Go after the suspect, Detective Knight. Park the sympathy. I'll be fine. Paul is still breathing. He is alive."

Penelope did as she was told. She ran into Dodge who was wrapping his red kerchief around his arm.

"I knew this kerchief was important. My dog likes the color. He brings me the kerchiefs in the morning. Davidson has a leg wound, too, like your husband. They seem to aim there except in my case. They don't know that I can shoot with either hand."

"Should we leave Davidson?"

Dodge nodded.

"I saw Barbara running after Cathy. There was a shot. The devil woman must be running out of bullets. I saw her gun brand. Let's run this way."

Penelope watched Dodge run forward. She followed him and caught up with him.

"Where are we headed?"

"Cathy is running for the open field. Either she has a helicopter or a car. The worst scenario might happen. She might take my bird. Someone could have shown or helped her bypass the lock."

They saw Barbara sitting near a tree. She was staunching a wound with her arm sleeves.

"I'm hit but not too bad. The bullet grazed my shoulder. You two detectives are a sight. Keep going."

She pointed toward the field. Dodge and Penelope were close to the open field. Dodge tripped and fell. He groaned. Penelope stopped to help him up.

They watched a strange red helicopter take off. A man was flying the machine. Cathy jumped in Dodge's helicopter and started the engine.

"Darn it!"

38 Airfield and Cathy

Dodge adjusted the red kerchief tie on his wounded arm.

"Don't chase a chopper with the blades twirling. The wind can suck you into the blade. I think I know where the two perps are headed. We must get to your vehicle."

Suddenly Hugh arrived and beeped the horn. He looked out of the large company car window. Penelope knew the car was the one with air conditioning problems.

"Need a ride? Carter and Susan are at the warehouse helping the police. The ambulances arrived, and they are taking the wounded to the hospital."

Penelope and Dodge joined him. Dodge sat in the back seat, and Penelope was in the front. She told Hugh the name of the airfield.

Hugh shook his head because he didn't understand which direction to drive. He threw up his hands in a gesture of unfamiliarity. Dodge hollered out the directions which made Hugh spin the tires as the car lurched forward.

They reached the small airfield.

"Drive the road to the right. The newbies use the number six slot to get refueled. We should try there first."

Hugh saw the gas pumps and stopped. Dodge stepped out of the car and staggered backward against the door.

"You stay put, Dodge. Penelope and I will go find Cathy. Make sure you keep a lookout for Simon."

"She's refueling at the sixth pump and acting as if nothing happened. How can she be so composed and unfeeling about her sister?"

Penelope made the mistake and pointed. Cathy saw her, dropped the hose, and fired her gun in rapid succession. She and Hugh hurriedly ducked behind two gas pumps.

"This isn't a safe place normally."

Penelope looked at the black tar. There was a rainbow rim which meant fuel where she was standing.

"Cut the jokes, Hugh."

The female detective saw the windsock which was flat.

"The air is nonexistent, and we are devoid of matter."

Her partner noticed the lack of wind.

Hugh said, "We are in a perfect vacuum."

She moved away from the pump. He started running ahead of her. Penelope ran faster, and her partner fell behind. She saw Cathy stop, turn, and raise her gun hand.

Penelope was in a direct line with the suspect. Her partner was off to her right. She heard Hugh yell the command for the suspect to stop and put down the weapon.

The image of the shooting range appeared in her view. The paper target matched the body in front of her. There was nothingness. Sound and everything around her fell away. The detective was in a life-or-death situation. Her training kicked in.

She saw Cathy bend her knees and move her left hand upward to support the handgun. The suspect was readying her stance and taking precise aim.

Penelope yelled, "Drop your weapon!"

The left hand on the suspect continued to rise.

"Nuts!"

With controlled movement, Penelope raised her gun rapidly as she ran and fired.

Cathy crumpled to the ground and didn't move. Penelope waited for Hugh to step beside her. She gasped for some air. Hugh did the same and wiped his brow with his hand. He leaned forward. His words were spoken with pauses in between.

"The suspect is down. Nice shot partner."

"I think she's dead. I aimed to maim but the look on her face and her stance told me differently. She was going to kill me."

"We hope she is dead. There must have been two shooters to have done the damage at the warehouse. Too bad we only downed one of the bad people," said Hugh.

"I killed her. There was no choice. She also shot Liam at the warehouse."

He looked around and back toward the pumps.

"Where's Simon?"

Penelope looked and glanced toward Dodge.

"He disappeared. We think the man was Simon. The windshield and helmet didn't give us a clear view. I'm not sure who was in the helicopter."

They heard sirens in the distance and saw police car lightbars. The flashing red and blue LED lights were a welcome sight.

"Finally, the police arrive. What happened to the bevy of police at the warehouse?" asked Penelope.

"We have a mole who called them away. Liam only had one man with him when he went inside while Dodge and Davidson stayed outside."

"I'm going to kill him when we get home."

Hugh again commented about the kill shot.

"You did good, detective. I haven't seen a running shot in some time. The suspect took a stand. There was no way out but down."

Penelope knew the tension at the scene dissipated.

"Come on. Let's check the dead perp."

Hugh kicked away Cathy's gun. With his gloves, he picked up the weapon and checked the clip.

"The suspect's gun shows three bullets left. Three bullets would have either maimed or killed you and me. We do have one very dead body."

Hugh mopped his face with a handkerchief.

"I'll stay here at the scene. You go back to Dodge and make sure he gets inside the ambulance."

Penelope looked one more time at Cathy.

"There's a total waste of a human being."

"I agree with your statement. We both told her to drop the weapon. I don't understand why she didn't. This young woman lived with the rich. Her family's lawyer would have kept her out of jail for some time."

Penelope looked over the airfield. The windsock lifted slightly. She didn't like killing people, especially someone younger than herself. She felt Jane was somehow with her in the final scene. The wayward daughter and her friends were responsible for the mind-boggling mess. Jane had every reason to not trust her sister. Penelope certainly didn't trust Cathy in those last seconds.

"Some things aren't about money. Cathy Blair was anti-social, anti-authority, and anti-family. The gang liked her viewpoint and free money. She didn't understand how deep they took her down until it was too late."

Hugh placed the handgun in an evidence bag.

"Tell Dodge he should take shooting lessons from you."

The detective put her gun away.

"When he isn't wounded, Dodge is better than me any day of the week. He would have dropped the suspect at the gas pump. I tried to buy her time to help change her mind."

Penelope left Hugh with the body. She reached the car and touched Dodge's shoulder. He turned slightly. Dodge also witnessed the scene as things continued to fall apart.

"I didn't see Simon. There was a guy who looked similar. His clothing was wrong. He wore a mechanics coverall. I should have made him stop. He disappeared behind a building. By the time I reached the corner, the stranger was gone. Simon probably flew somewhere else. I'm glad you practiced shooting recently. When I returned to the vehicle, you dropped the suspect while running. Excellent move, detective."

She leaned against the car emotionally exhausted. Tears filled her eyes. They spilled like a dam breaking.

Dodge took Penelope in his arms and handed her a different handkerchief.

"I hate it when women cry. I think I'm responsible. I know I am."

"You are not responsible for me, Dodge."

"Go ahead and give yourself a minute. This isn't like the Allan Duran incident in New York City. Duran was trapped and took a bullet. You happened to be trapped, too, by an awfully bad man. Your fiancée died because he loved you. Liam was trapped and got out of the way. He can be fast. Besides, we know he loves you. I can see the love in his face whenever I'm around both of my friends."

Penelope hugged Dodge for trying to cheer her up and re-focus her energy.

"He never should have been in the warehouse with one man."

"You and I understand the danger. Liam does his thing. He reacts. There's no fear in him when he is on the job. The warehouse scene could have been worse. Maybe someone should talk to him."

39 One Queen Down and the Aftermath

Liam called her on her cell phone. Penelope was thankful until she thought about what Dodge told her. She bristled with anger.

"Since when do you go into a warehouse with one policeman. Are you crazy? You told me we're supposed to be careful. You weren't careful at all."

"Detective Knight, I need to have your report."

Penelope halted in her tirade. Her boss was pushing. A brief report is what she decided to hand over as her answer.

"Cathy's dead; my shot. Simon or whoever the person was escaped."

She waited for his reply. There was none and she softened.

"Liam, what were you thinking?"

Dodge was pleased she was giving Liam a piece of her mind, and then she softened. The woman was back to normal. Penelope recovered from the shooting of a dangerous suspect. She was a darn good detective in his mind. He smiled and refused the ambulance.

Carter and Susan appeared. Penelope disconnected from her call and joined the loud group. Carter argued his point and made Dodge feel even guiltier about not getting in the ambulance.

"Okay, okay. I'll have the EMT's take me to the emergency room. Which hospital is Liam in? Maybe we can order takeout and get a discount."

Penelope was glad Dodge jumped inside the ambulance. The ambulance pulled away. She turned and waved to Hugh. Hugh shook hands with the policeman at the death scene and walked back. They left Susan with him. Penelope and Carter drove to the hospital.

At the hospital, she waited until her husband was wheeled from the recovery room. The nurse informed her that she could enter the small private room as the interns rolled her husband there. After they left, she talked with Liam in his hospital bed.

"The nurse went to look for a leg brace. I have nothing bad happening inside the leg. The bullet was clean and is out. I can go once the doctor checks me out as normal. Paul Beeker is in surgery. He told me he followed his wife to the warehouse. Davidson will be out for two weeks. His leg is worse. Dodge called me, and said the ambulance found Barbara. He said the shot in his arm hurt like a bear bite. I think he is here in the ER."

Penelope handed her husband the water jug with the straw. She touched his cheek and withdrew her hand.

"Jane followed Cathy to warehouse one. She was suspicious of her sister. I'm sorry Jane didn't survive. Paul will be, too, once he knows the whole story. She knew about Cathy's drone project or at least she guessed. Cathy used her sister for the gang's purposes. Jane knew because she was asked to set up the tour. Jane was afraid to tell Paul about the tour and the other stuff. I think she thought she could fix her sister if given time."

Liam motioned the nurse who put on his brace. She made him stand.

"The brace fits fine. Get the doctor, please."

Penelope saw Liam grimace.

"I saw the broken box and drone parts on the floor. We were right about the shipment. The drones were important and were hidden in the container."

The doctor came in and signed the paperwork.

Liam stood with his new brace.

"Shall we see if Dodge needs a ride back to the airfield? They should have cleared his helicopter by now. You were right about the Container 10 contents. Our captain was pleased except for the injuries. They have a bulletin out for Simon's arrest. I think he's going to be harder to catch, but we have some ideas."

Penelope handed Liam his crutches.

"Good thing you've used these before."

They stopped in the emergency room to pick up Dodge.

Liam grabbed the nearest stool. Dodge nodded to Penelope and spoke.

"Barbara's husband took her home. Hugh and Susan have left the airfield. Carter is back at the office, and Davidson's wife arrived to take him home. The body of Cathy Blair is on the way to the same morgue as Jane Beeker's body. I'm the last person you must drop off. In the morning, I can take my dog home to recuperate from the vet. If I see the Simon dude, I'm going to shove some rats down his throat."

"Thanks for the update, Dodge. Sorry about your dog."

"He's a tough critter like me."

They made sure Dodge flew his helicopter and arrived home. He probably shouldn't have flown but couldn't be swayed. He said something about juveniles writing graffiti if he didn't move. The bird went over their heads at the airfield. The sun was already high in the sky.

"The feds showed up and checked everything on Dodge's helicopter. I told them they could go. The bird checked out fine. They recommended a change with the ignition start capability."

"What about the mole?"

"He's thankfully been arrested. The police will hold the warehouse until they are done collecting evidence and taken pictures."

"Where does this put Paul Beeker?"

Liam thought for a minute.

"I'm sure he and his lawyer will be glad to help us find Simon. Beeker's lawyer arranged warehouse one for Cathy Blair. He created a paper party business for her and arranged the warehouse for her paper product company."

"She used everybody."

Liam was glad they reached the office. Carter came out and talked with Liam. He and Susan were the furthest away from the action.

"I told him the bust was a success despite the missing police. At least we had four detectives unhurt. He wanted me to congratulate you on your long shot. We can go home now. I think you should drive, detective wife."

"Yes, sir, Detective Knight."

She pulled out of the parking lot a little too fast.

"Your sports car moves faster than mine."

Liam laid his head on the headrest.

"She is exquisite."

"How exquisite?"

He glanced at his wife.

"Penelope, no."

She put her pedal down, and the car leaped. He held on until she slowed to normal speed.

"You are bad and brave."

Her brown eyes glanced at his.

"I'm taking a short nap," said Liam.

"Good. I can make spaghetti when we get home."

"Something soft will work fine. My pills should be ready"

Penelope turned west off the freeway toward the beach.

"They've already put the prescription in our mailbox. I explained we needed a special delivery."

"Perfect."

Penelope helped him inside the beach house. She quickly cooked the spaghetti and heated the frozen sauce. She brought him a water bottle, pills, and a plate of food. He laid down and fell asleep. Penelope returned to the kitchen and sat in the lounge chair until he awoke.

"My leg hurts something fierce."

She handed him some more pills.

"Jonathan called. He wanted to make sure you are better after your surgery."

"I'm getting there. I do need massive hugs."

Penelope slid next to him.

"You fired the shot running?"

“I did. There was a moment when I hesitated, but our extensive training took over. She wouldn’t put down the gun. Dodge or Hugh told you about the shot.”

“Dodge did. The bullet hit the mark. She was gone instantly. Remind me to walk behind you when you have a gun in your hand.”

Penelope thought about the female killer.

“I was pissed she shot my husband.”

“I promise not to piss you off ever again.”

Liam put his arm around his wife. The day was finally over, and he was relieved.

She squeezed his arm and thought about Simon. The man was minus a partner. From watching the man flee in the helicopter, she was able to assess his character more. The man would run for cover and let others take the fall. She saw the black car that followed her and Susan from the Beeker’s house and when the car swerved toward her while she was walking to the deli.

“I think Simon was the driver in the black vehicle or possibly someone working with him.”

Liam called Jonathan and told him.

“He may have dumped the vehicle. If the person is someone else, let’s hope they aren’t as smart. At least the police can look for something more specific. The witnesses in the shops also thought the driver was a man.”

“Do you think Simon might come after us? You are the lead investigator.”

Liam shifted his arm.

“I need to walk some.”

He took a single crutch and seemed able to maneuver on the first floor. She watched as he navigated around the room. Liam halted.

"From now on, we go to work together. I drive because I'm better at shifting."

Penelope agreed that Liam was a better driver. His arms weren't wounded. Getting out of a car spin was not her thing.

40 Status and Substitution

Hugh was with Penelope and Liam at his home. Emma took the kids out of the house for a tennis shoe and a new shorts outfit shopping trip. She guaranteed they would be gone three hours.

"We're having ribs, coleslaw, and tater tots for supper."

Liam handed Hugh a large bottle of barbeque sauce.

"You stopped at Blubber's Place. I love his homemade sauce."

"Emma told Penelope you were almost out. Your wife didn't want you to try your recipe again."

"My wife doesn't like my sauce?"

Penelope and Liam grinned.

"Neither do we."

"My heart is broken."

Hugh opened the sauce bottle and poured some sauce on a large spoon. He tasted.

"Oh, this is way better."

Hugh put the bottle in the refrigerator.

"I'll freeze some. I don't trust my kids. They spill a lot. Where are we with the Simon-dude to paraphrase Dodge. At least he and Davidson are having a good time on vacation."

Liam proceeded with his status report.

"We checked with the firm he was going to join after leaving the Beeker's. We're not looking at avionics or software. Our focus was on engineering. The CEO authorized the release of names and their resumes for us to preview once we presented him with a warrant. We've narrowed our focus to four men. Currently, they are being watched. None of them owns a black vehicle that we know. This leads me to wonder if we selected the wrong specialty. We've also monitored Simon's parent's home. Nothing unusual has happened at his former home. We've checked Cathy's credit cards with Paul Beeker's approval. Again, nothing there. She had many checking accounts all over the city."

Hugh didn't look happy.

"Surely, the helicopter revealed something."

"Per Penelope and Dodge, they remembered the numbers on the helicopter. The numbers were bogus."

"We have illegal drone making and an illegal helicopter, not to mention the transport of goods illegally. Why aren't the feds helping us?"

Liam shrugged.

"Their resources are as limited as ours. Right now, they think this is our fight. We have no idea if the cameras or controllers are illegally made outside of California."

Hugh passed the sugar cookies around.

"We have checked with the drone manufacturers?"

Liam sighed.

"We did early on, and we did again. There was total silence. At least they have been warned about Simon."

"We could borrow some military parts."

Liam's brain started clicking.

"Good idea, Hugh."

Penelope was taken aback when Liam pulled out some pages. He handed her the notes.

"Hugh has been working with Carter and the police. They've been looking at storage garages for the black car."

Penelope read the paper.

"You found the car."

"We think we have found the car."

Penelope looked between Hugh and her husband.

"There's a plan for the car. That's why the secrecy in getting us to your house. We went on a boat ride to a dock where Emma and the kids picked us up."

"We have found a black sports car like mine. There are police people dressed like you and me. They are going to take a leisurely drive to San Diego to see if anyone follows them today."

Penelope hoped the plan worked.

Liam grabbed her hand and kissed her fingers.

"If the plan doesn't work today, we will try again."

"If you two lovebirds will excuse me, I have to light the grill."

Liam relinquished her fingers.

"I should help. We don't need to feed the firemen today."

"I heard that," said Hugh.

Liam walked outside and watched Hugh.

"How's Dodge's dog?"

He petted his female dog.

"She misses his visits. Dodge comes over on occasion."

"Per Dodge, the dog appears healthy. We should have him over more often."

"It's okay. Emma and the kids like Dodge. He's like their grandpa."

"I wouldn't tell Dodge that name. He doesn't think that his age shows."

"Not to worry. I corrected my kids. First, I threatened no cookies. I finally used no ice cream."

Liam helped him find the wood smoke in the garage. They put the wood chips in foil and returned to the grill. Hugh fanned the wood smoke fire. The smoke drifted over the fence.

"I thought by now we would have heard your neighbor complain."

"They moved."

Liam wondered about the old neighbor. There would be no one to bother his detective. Hugh shrugged.

"I have no idea why. The house has been on the market for three months."

Liam looked at Hugh. Hugh turned red in the face.

"Why hasn't the house sold?"

Hugh worded his answer carefully.

"My dog goes for a walk."

"I did see the light spots on the lawn, and their grass looked terrible in places."

Hugh moved the container for the wood smoke.

"It is time."

The men went to the kitchen and grabbed two pans of ribs. Hugh rubbed oil on the barbeque bars. The men put the meat pans on the grill.

"We cook them low and slow. The neighbor's fenced backyard is green."

Liam knew Hugh was talking in riddles.

"I give. Why isn't the front yard green?"

Hugh's dog came over and spit out a red object. Liam bent down. He petted the dog. Liam knew the red plastic was the flow cap on the watering tubes. Hugh filled some dog containers with water from the hose.

"Doesn't anyone check the watering system?"

Hugh put salt and pepper on the ribs and shut the top.

"The watering system runs at night. I tried to tell the old fool the morning was better. Would you like to get a good deal on a nice house with a fixable yard?"

Liam and Penelope weren't ready for a house or children.

"No, we aren't ready. My beach house and the condo are enough. Have you talked to Dodge?"

"He looked at the house last week."

Now Liam was paying attention. He opened the lid. The fire under the pans was the right height, and the temperature gauge the correct heat.

"And?"

Hugh said, "We should go into the house. I'll set the timer for forty minutes before we turn them."

They went into the house. The doorbell rang. Liam went to the door. There stood Dodge with his dog. The dog bolted. Hugh was in the back of the house holding the door open for the dog to enter the backyard. They heard the two dogs welcoming each other.

Dodge stepped inside and shook hands with Hugh.

"Hi, neighbor, the house is mine next Friday." Penelope looked at the three detectives. "I missed something."

41 Interview with Driver

The two detectives waited for the prisoner in a private room. The man was brought to the room and lock ironed to the table. The jailors left the room.

Liam introduced himself and Carter to the prisoner. He explained the reason for their visit.

"I need to explain that a man you know is responsible for eight murders, five wounded, and a woman and her sister's death. I have three photographs that I will show you. If you can point out your friend, I guarantee your evening meal will be better than yesterday."

"They fed me seafood yesterday. I told them I was allergic. The police are trying to kill me."

"Mr. Ames. Your attention is required. The photographs are in front of you," said Liam as he pointed.

The man fingered the photos.

"This one here. This is the man who hired me to follow and scare a woman."

Liam had placed three different photographs. Two were actors and the other one was an altered photo of Simon with a beard. The man selected their altered photograph. The police would have a better idea of what to look for."

"Thank you, Mr. Ames." Liam waited and sat still.

The man looked around the room. Carter watched the prisoner.

"Your man is staring at me and you stopped talking."

"I stopped talking because I'm sure you have a lot of questions."

The man looked vaguely at Liam. Liam was encouraged.

"You seem like a smart man. I'm certain you might know where we can find the man in the picture. However, I know that I shouldn't ask. Your lawyer isn't present."

Mr. Ames grunted.

"What lawyer? I didn't see a lawyer yesterday or today."

Liam knew the man received no visitors.

"The last prisoner my colleague Mr. Carter met with was given a plastic vile of narcotics. Unfortunately, the prisoner died. We hope someone hasn't given you a vile recently."

Mr. Ames relinquished the plastic vile he was hiding under his arm. He placed the vile on the table.

"Mr. Ames, you are lucky today that we came to visit you."

The prisoner nodded.

"I don't like taking any kind of medicine, so I figured no one would know if I took the stuff or not. Faking an illness might work better."

Carter bagged the plastic vile very carefully with a gloved hand. The prisoner noticed.

"We have to be careful. The outside could be as deadly as the inside," prompted Liam.

The prisoner suddenly looked afraid. He looked at his armpit with caution. He started talking.

"I get a new uniform when they put me back."

Liam nodded.

"I met the man in a bar called Smithy's Den. He told me he lived in the neighborhood. I followed him. He didn't live there. He stepped in this expensive car and drove off. Then he came back and showed me cash for a job. He gave me keys and hired a taxi so I could go to the storage yard. The gas tank was full. I did the job. End of story until he showed up a second and third time which you probably know about."

Liam was pleased the prisoner talked.

"What color, model, and make was the car the man drove?"

"Dark blue. Not a medium size. The car was smaller. I saw part of the license number, *DBR*."

"Good. Can you tell me the date and the name of the taxi?"

The prisoner tried to remember.

"I think a month or two ago. Days come and go when there are no jobs. I don't keep track. The cab was the orange one with large numbers on top. The name escapes me."

Liam knew the cab company.

"Is there anything else you can tell us about the man?"

Mr. Ames watched the air vent.

"There's a cobweb. This place is full of spiders."

Liam knew he was losing the interview. He spoke softly.

"Mr. Ames, please. You saw something important. At the time, you noticed."

Carter was impressed with Liam's firm voice and patience.

"He wore a ring on his right hand. I wondered if the ring was real gold. I don't know many people who wear gold."

"The man wore a wedding ring?"

The prisoner shook his head.

Liam dug his small notebook out of his pocket and ripped off a page. He slid the paper and ink pen to the man.

"A drawing might be easier to show us."

Mr. Ames toyed with the paper rolling the edges. He picked up the pen. Carter was fascinated. The man drew a circle. Then he drew a small head with whiskers. When he was done, the prisoner shoved the drawing and pen back to Liam.

Liam pocketed the pen and drawing.

"I appreciate your time, Mr. Ames. They promised me the evening meal would be fried chicken with mashed potatoes, gravy, and corn this evening. The dessert is a butterscotch cake. I'll ask for new coveralls and a shower."

The prisoner nodded.

"The meal sounds enjoyable. My underarm itches. I should go shower and change."

Liam motioned to the guard and put in the two requests. The prisoner was taken away. The two men exited the room and the jail building. Liam walked to their company car, and Carter followed.

"The picture the prisoner drew for the ring was something I didn't understand."

Liam started the car.

"The ring belongs to a gang."

Carter wasn't sure if they needed to add a gang to this case.

"I've seen this ring a long time ago when I first started as a detective. Hugh will know the drawing as will Dodge. The gang society was very hidden and hard to find. We got lucky in catching one of them."

Carter blew out his breath.

"Shit."

Liam was in total agreement. The drawing changed things by a magnitude of one hundred. He pulled into the parking lot and gave their attendant the keys and car.

"We thought the gang disbanded. I'm going to have to talk with our boss. Tell Penelope that I'll be longer than planned."

Carter watched Liam walk up the steps to the building door. Penelope and Barbara drove into the parking lot. He detained Penelope and told her about the interview. Carter left.

Penelope went inside. She busied herself at her desk until Liam came out.

"Carter told me. Have you told Hugh and Dodge?"

"They know."

"I've read a lot about gangs. This one I don't know. However, they usually follow the same stupid rules. I might be able to help."

Liam made a strange suggestion.

"You might want to visit your mom and dad for a couple of weeks. Jonathan will approve the time off."

"Are you going with me?"

"No."

Penelope was confused. Her husband held up his hand.

"We can talk at home. There might be something we can do to change our odds. But with this gang reactivated, some alterations are required."

42 Old Farmhouse

An old pickup stopped in the yard. Two geese squawked and ran when the man opened his door. He looked at the vehicles parked next to the old farmhouse. The man could smell eggs cooking. He opened the broken screen door. The paint peeled off a long time ago. The man hated the old farmhouse. The place was too dull and too quiet.

Simon saw the man and put a plate of eggs on the table. The man took a fork out of the drawer. He stood and ate his eggs. Throwing the empty plate and fork in the sink, the plastic clattered.

"Tell me about this deal you heard about through your golden grapevine."

Simon flipped the eggs, salted the tops, and waited thirty seconds. Sliding the cooked eggs onto a second plate, he turned the burner off the stove. He ignored the man for the moment and ate the soft eggs savoring each bite. He also threw his plate in the sink.

"Jason, clean up this mess. I'm going outside."

Simon and the man walked to a small creek that went through the property. The creek was the only clean thing on the property.

"An engineer I know told me about someone selling military-grade cameras and controllers. We need those parts. Our other supplier bailed."

The man kicked at a tuft of grass.

"I don't like this idea. We're missing cameras and controllers, and they suddenly appear on the black market. The deal sounds rigged to me."

Simon looked at the stream of water. The sand was the same sand he saw the day before. He was bored with seeing the sand.

"Cathy used to supply us with money. With her out of the picture, we need to move."

The man broke a blade of grass off and twisted the tassel.

"How much are these people asking?"

"Fifty thousand dollars."

The man shredded the piece of grass.

"The price seems reasonable. You could save money and buy the parts from a manufacturer. How much money is left?"

"We have ten thousand. Don't worry. I'll only show them the top part of the money. I don't want plain parts. We discussed this same issue before."

The two men walked to the pickup. The man spoke.

"I'm moving to Oregon. There's a job as a forklift operator at a small company. Here is my new phone number. Do you think you can remember the number?"

Simon rubbed some dirt off the truck.

"My brain still works. I know you stopped working for the Star Company. Too bad. The pay from the ships was good money."

"Working on the ships was getting too dangerous. I heard the police were snooping around again."

Simon looked at the farmhouse.

"As soon as we put the swarm drones together and sell them, we will move out of this place. I'll call you. You will receive your fair share."

The man opened the truck door.

"Call me once only. I don't need the money. We are over. I started this club. You can have everything. There's no fun in pursuing the drone project permanently without Cathy's money and the free warehouse."

Simon wanted to ask.

"About the day those other Beeker people died, I tried calling you all day and in the evening. You never answered. Then there was your friend who was a worker on the ship. No one has seen him. I asked some dockworkers at a pub. They told me your friend was saving his money for a small boat. There was no reason for him to not stick around if you get my drift. It's funny the worker was my same height, build, and hair color."

The man answered, "People died, big deal."

"There's also a small freezer missing from the barn. A person could fit a cow in there or a body. You also accidentally dropped my phone and broke the device. I appreciated your phone but was forced to remember a new number. I'm your stepbrother. You wouldn't lie to me about those dead people."

The man looked at the steep hill. Nothing moved except a hawk was flying overhead. The hawk knew where to find food. He didn't owe Simon any explanation.

"You needed a new phone. I obliged. The cops track phones, and too many people knew your old number. I hauled the freezer to the dump. The cord was frayed. The worker returned to Mexico would be my guess. Or he fell off the ship. The ocean gets rough and choppy. Then there are the engine propellers. Workers are easy to replace if they lose their balance."

Simon didn't like the explanations. There wasn't much he could do. People did die every day. He should probably not mention the dead people again.

The man stared him in the eyes. The look was distant and strange.

"Don't ever go to a dock pub again."

Simon knew his stepbrother was one scary dude. His last comment told him the truth.

"What about your helicopter."

"The helicopter is being repainted. For now, I will leave the helicopter where she is stored. The bird is too hot to sell. In a year or two, I'll sell or take it apart. I haven't decided. My car has been exchanged for another one."

"You aren't even upset about Cathy."

The man watched the hawk swoop to the earth.

"Sure, I'm upset. Someone should pay for our business loss. We put the time in the project, and they intervened."

Simon's eyes followed the man as he drove down the dusty road. He went inside and picked the men who would go with him.

In the bedroom, he readied the briefcase with the fake money and eight- thousand dollars of the real money. He tossed his new girlfriend two thousand dollars.

"Hide this money for me. Don't lose any of the bills."

He watched her stuff the money inside an envelope and tape the money to a bottom drawer.

"If I don't call, you can take off. Leave the money."

His woman asked who the man was that visited the farm.

"The man is no one. If anyone asks, he was never here."

The woman left him alone.

Simon went out to the crumbling barn and looked at the boxes of drone bodies and propellers. He could sell the parts and leave. The money wouldn't be the same amount. With the camera and controllers, the drones would be more valuable.

He debated about his choices.

"The risk was high."

He grabbed his gun on the workbench and checked the chamber. The gun was his favorite. Simon took three larger weapons off the wall and carried them to the car. He saw the wire holding the bumper was loose. He bent and twisted the wire tighter.

Simon checked the license plate. This plate was stolen the prior evening off a dealer's lot of used cars. The plate should be okay for a few more days.

He walked into the house.

"Jason, get those devices put together. We don't have all day."

Jason went out to the barn. He fed the geese before making the devices. Simon's woman joined him. She watched as he tinkered.

"Will these drones work?"

Jason looked at the boxes. "They will fly."

"I have to go home for a day. My clothes need washing. There are no machines in a laundromat within ten miles of this place."

Jason watched the woman walk. Simon joined him.

"Are we slow today? Stop staring at my girlfriend," said Simon.

Jason stopped putting the device together. His concentration was jarred.

"I can't make these today."

Simon grabbed him by the neck.

"You will finish them or else."

"I'll try. Steve is the bomb expert. Let go of me."

"Steve left. I'm in charge now. His name has been stricken from the books."

"Oh, man. I need him."

Simon saw his girlfriend put the clothes basket in her car. He strolled over to talk with her. His mood was nasty.

"Put the clothes in the house. I need you to stay here and watch the place, especially the stuff in the barn."

"My clothes are dirty."

"Wash them in the creek, or there's a rusty tub out back."

She stormed into the house, grabbed the dish soap, and took her laundry basket. He watched her wash and hang her clothes on the line.

Simon felt a headache coming on. He sneezed.

"I hate grass, dust, geese, and idiots."

He stepped in duck droppings.

"Shit."

Simon went inside the house. The rest of his men were taking a nap. He was restless and couldn't sleep. He went outside and sat in the car playing the radio. The battery went dead.

"Jason!"

"What?"

"Fix this battery."

Jason threw up his hands.

43 Montana and Set-Up

Penelope waited with her husband for Dodge to arrive with his dog. Dodge handed over the leash.

"Hi, Dodge, I'm ready."

She turned to Liam.

"Are you sure?"

Liam held his wife gently in his arms and kissed her. They made the decision together the prior evening.

"I am sure. Call me when you arrive. Tell your mom and dad I appreciate the short notice for your visit."

"I will. Watch your back."

Dodge tucked her in his truck. "Make sure your head is down until we get out of town. At this point, we aren't sure if anyone is watching."

After thirty minutes Dodge tapped her head. Penelope sat in her seat.

"We'll be arriving at the private airfield shortly. Then I'll move my bird closer to Hugh's place."

Penelope put her bag in the helicopter. He flew her to San Francisco and went with her as far as he could go to catch her flight to Billings, Montana. He watched her airplane take off. Dodge used his phone.

"She's on her way."

Dodge went back to his helicopter which was refueled. He headed south to Los Angeles. Dodge picked up Liam.

"There's been no disturbance since you left. Either they are busy gathering money or they are cleaning their guns."

"I doubt they will bring all the money."

Liam knew Dodge was probably correct. They drove to Dodge's new property next to Hugh's place. When they drove in the driveway, Hugh and Carter were waiting with their gear of tools.

Liam looked at Hugh.

"Emma and the kids left. She's visiting her parents with our dog and Dodge's dog. I purchased a new fence for Emma's parents last week."

Carter, I need your report," said Liam.

"Susan went with a friend on vacation to Hawaii, and Barbara is flying to Miami with her husband. The female detectives are out of the building."

"Gentlemen, we need to set the cameras. Let's get started. We are glad Dodge has offered his house for the fake stakeout."

Dodge watched as the men dropped their gear.

"I hate this wallpaper. Who puts peaches in a kitchen?"

Hugh looked.

"I think those are pale raspberries."

"Raspberries? They make me think of bears. Because Jonathan has agreed to pay for repairs, I'll be okay with any damage."

Liam stepped away and took a call.

"Hey, you've landed; and your father and the chauffeur are taking you to the ranch. Great. I'll talk with you later this evening. We're working the set."

The men worked for two hours. Dodge was tired.

"We have the fence gate to complete."

Liam noticed his friend was rubbing his eyes.

"How about you take a short nap. The three of us can manage a gate. If it's crooked, you can fix the gate tomorrow."

Dodge laid down on the couch. The three detectives worked with the electric saw to cut out part of the fence. Carter dug a new post hole. They screwed the gate into the post, installed the latch, and tested the gate. Hugh checked the level.

"We're done."

The men put the tools in the large bags and carried them over to Hugh's garage.

"I still think we should install a pit just in case the other stuff fails," suggested Hugh.

Liam looked at Hugh's neat garage.

"We burn some burgers and talk about where to put the pit."

Hugh and Carter slapped their hands at each other.

"I don't mind being the first person to dig the pit," said Carter.

Dodge joined them.

"I used to be a gravedigger."

The three men laughed hilariously. Hugh led them through the gate. Dodge shut the gate.

"Not bad for the first time."

He followed the detectives inside. Hugh took out the huge mound of hamburger from his refrigerator in the kitchen. The men washed their hands in the laundry room and made large patties.

Hugh looked at the buns. He was glad Emma bought the large size from the bakery.

"We're having potato chips, dip, and macaroni salad. The kids made the salad in case you find anything strange. The dog ate most of the stuff that fell on the floor."

Carter wasn't used to being around Hugh.

"He's kidding," said Liam.

"No, he's not," intervened Dodge. "Because the floor is sticky."

Hugh took a paper towel and washed the floor.

"The ants have been moving."

Hugh snuck a small, sweet pickle from the jar and placed the pickle in Carter's bowl. He put the bowls of macaroni on the table. The forks were passed around.

"No eating until the burgers are done."

Hugh disappeared to cook the meat on the grill. Carter went with him.

Dodge and Liam looked at Carter's macaroni salad.

"Are you thinking what I'm thinking?"

Liam nodded.

"The man is a picky eater. I grabbed a jalapeno off the bush outside."

"Let me see."

"The jalapeno is the same size as the sweet pickle. We need to dump the stem."

Liam cut the stem off. They switched the pickle out for the jalapeno.

"What do we do with the pickle?" asked Liam.

Dodge stuck the pickle in Hugh's macaroni.

"You know at some point they are going to get even with us."

Liam was content with a possible revenge match.

"We can stand the heat."

The burgers were brought inside and placed on the table. Hugh passed around plastic glasses, paper plates, and put the milk jug on the table.

"No need for fancy, right?"

The men helped themselves to the sesame seed buns, chip, and dip. The burgers were grabbed, and the milk was poured. Liam went to the refrigerator and took out the chocolate syrup. He poured some in his milk and tossed the syrup to Dodge. Hugh squeezed mustard on his meat.

"Any horseradish?"

"Liam, you know the jar is in the refrigerator."

Dodge went to get the jar and grabbed the ketchup. He squeezed some on his burgers.

"I saw a red onion in the refrigerator," commented Liam.

"Oh, for Pete's sake."

Hugh went and sliced some thin red onion. He plopped the onions on a plate and put the plate in the center of the table.

Dodge and Liam grabbed some onions. They all watched while Carter helped himself to a large bite of macaroni salad. His eyes bulged, and he swallowed.

Drinking a glass of milk, he coughed twice and appeared to recover. Hugh ate a large bite of macaroni and spit out the pickle which landed on top of Carter's hamburger bun. Carter took the bun off and put it aside. The pickle rolled under Hugh's favorite chair in the living room.

"Okay, wise guys, what did Carter eat?"

Dodge and Liam were in tears of laughter.

"A jalapeno."

Hugh chuckled.

Carter ate the rest of the macaroni salad. During the night he went to the refrigerator and blew out the insides of the first eight eggs.

Hugh came down and saw the last egg blow job.

"It's a good thing Emma bought extra eggs. They are in the refrigerator in the garage. She's used to Dodge and Liam's pranks. Welcome to the group."

Carter was glad he was considered a part of the group.

In the morning, Hugh sat in his favorite chair with a cup of coffee. He noticed a few ants. Hugh knew about ants. A few ants turned into a freaking tornado of ants crawling everywhere. He went into the kitchen and grabbed the ant killer spray.

Dodge came down.

"I believe they are after the pickle."

Dodge went outside and brought a new carton of eggs inside.

"I usually stomp on them. There's no harmful spray."

Liam came down, helped move the chair, and tossed the pickle in the garbage disposal.

"Okay, contest time. Dodge stomps and Hugh will spray. Whoever kills the most ants will win the pot."

"What do I win?" asked Dodge.

Liam laid down a ten-dollar bill.

"Liam's a cheapskate, but Hugh, you are on. I've drunk my coffee. It was nice of Emma to put those K-things in my room."

Dodge stomped and Hugh sprayed.

Carter came downstairs.

"Man, it stinks in here. Did you hear the thunder?"

Dodge cracked the eggs in a bowl and pocketed the ten. Carter looked in the refrigerator. All the blown-out eggs were missing.

Dodge pointed to the garbage can.

"I won the ant killing contest."

Carter's mouth dropped open.

"Don't ask. This is a sore point for someone in a chair in the other room," said Liam.

"I heard that."

Liam took the sausage patties out of the freezer and put them in a pan. He turned the stove dial.

Hugh returned the ant poison under the laundry room sink. He washed his hands. Hugh surveyed his turf.

"Carter, start the toast."

Hugh threw him a loaf of bread.

Sitting down in his chair again, Hugh was going to take a sip of his coffee. Liam refilled his cup.

"Thank you, Liam. I almost won. The spray died. Call me when breakfast is ready."

Hugh opened his newspaper. Part of the newspaper was wet from the sprinkler system and the newspaper boy's throw.

"Normal day so far."

Liam flipped the sausage, and Dodge poured the scrambled egg mixture in the pan of heated butter. Carter was four toasts down, working on four more.

Liam grabbed the butter tub and a knife.

"The toast needs butter. Men need fat to survive. Fat builds muscles."

Carter started buttering.

"Emma left a jar of strawberry jelly in my room."

Dodge and Liam stopped cooking. They stared at Carter.

"I'll get the jelly."

"Did Emma leave anything in your room," asked Dodge. "I got dandelions from the kids and a hand-drawn picture of their dog missing an ear. There was a pink piece of eraser in the spot."

Liam looked out the kitchen window.

"A fern plant about eighteen inches tall was on a dresser. The pot looked homemade."

"Oh, no, not the darn fern plant. Maybe we could plant the thing in the garden and get a geranium for a replacement. Emma likes geraniums. I've seen some pretty ones at Clayton's Greenhouse. They call them double blooming or ever-blooming. I can't remember. We could buy a nice one."

The men ate their breakfast. Carter and Hugh did the dishes.

A delivery truck stopped near the front door and rang the bell. Dodge answered and paid the man. The two men switched out the plants. They took the fern into the backyard and planted it in the shade under a tree.

"Should we add some sticks for support?"

Liam didn't know anything about ferns.

"Penelope's ferns don't have any sticks. She does put fertilizer on them."

They stared at the fern. Each one remembered the bag in the garage.

"My guess is a no on the fertilizer."

Liam clapped Dodge on the back.

"Smart man."

They put the shovel and garden tools in the garage. Dodge turned the fertilizer bag around so a person couldn't read the label.

"Were we supposed to water the fern?"

Liam smiled evilly.

"The weather mentioned rain next week. Tuesday or Wednesday is when water will drop."

"Good enough for me. Sometimes the weather people are wrong. The frost came early last year."

Liam was having a good time.

"Penelope keeps telling me good things come in twos or were her words different? Let me think. Do bad things come in threes? I must be getting old as you, Dodge, I can't remember the simple stuff."

Dodge shoved him.

"I'm not old. I remember the simple stuff fine. We bought an ever-blooming geranium."

Liam wondered about the name. Dodge took the receipt out of his pocket from the greenhouse.

"You owe me half."

Liam stared at the receipt. The name of the plant was on the paper.

"You cheated. You read the receipt."

Dodge chuckled. "I left Emma a note regarding the plant exchange. I do want to get invited back for dinner in the future now that we are neighbors."

44 First Takedown

Hugh watched as Carter and Liam finished making their French bread meat sandwiches around nine-thirty in the morning. Liam placed the sandwiches in plastic bags, and Carter washed the knife.

"Dodge went downstairs to my bunker to check if the cameras we installed yesterday work. The police have military-grade cameras and controllers. They should be arriving next door with the boxes shortly."

Liam put the sandwiches and some colas in a small cooler.

"We are ready. The letters were delivered yesterday morning to our targeted engineers. We hope they passed the information to Simon's team. Dodge moved his truck in case we need to make a fast exit."

The men went down the steps to Hugh's basement. He knocked on a door, and Dodge opened the bunker room. Inside were computers and large screens. On the walls were guns, clips, and ammunition of various sizes and types. Hugh handed the others their riot gear and bulletproof vests.

"The captain wanted us to be well-prepared. How nice of him! He's back on my Christmas card list," said Dodge.

Carter walked around the room with a silly grin on his face.

"This is fantastic. Some of these guns must be yours."

"Emma's dad was into guns."

Dodge saw a car drive down the street.

"We have visual and sound. That is the last one of your neighbors to exit the area. He put three carriers in the car."

Hugh nodded, "My neighbor was delayed catching the cats. He borrowed a can of tuna this morning around five. He was afraid to fly the drone."

Liam was pleased with their preparations.

"The police special force should be in place. The paddy wagon is standing close by."

Dodge watched a screen intently.

"We have a vehicle making a third trip past the house. The vehicle has stopped."

"Two men are walking toward the house. The vehicle is backing up slowly," mentioned Hugh.

"The mice have arrived," said Dodge into the microphone.

The three policemen in the house responded. Liam watched as a man stepped out of the vehicle and went into the house next door. The two men inside the vehicle stepped outside. Hugh zoomed on the camera and pulled up the other men's faces.

"We have a problem. These men aren't Simon's group."

Carter looked at the mug shots.

"You are right. What do we do?"

Dodge was calm.

"We arrest the three engineers."

They watched as the swat team snuck in place. The man walked out of the house with two boxes. The men grabbed the boxes and put them in the vehicle. The man went back into the house and was arrested. The two outside gave up when the swat team showed their faces and guns.

The detectives went outside and watched as the paddy wagon stopped. The three men were placed inside.

The military came and retrieved their drone parts boxes. The police withdrew and left.

"We should take the cameras down and lock the house," said Dodge.

Liam was upset they didn't catch Simon. Dodge moved his truck into his driveway.

"I vote we eat those sandwiches in the cooler which is in the bunker."

The men returned to the bunker and slowly ate their sandwiches. Hugh opened the two bags of corn chips. He went upstairs to get the guacamole.

The men ate the gold and blue corn chips and dip. The time was two o'clock.

"We should wait for another hour, and then call it quits. The school bus arrives at around four o'clock."

Liam thought about the engineers.

"The market for illegal drone parts is higher than we expected. I imagine there are a lot of competitors in the game. Simon and his gang must know quite a few of them. We keep thinking Simon killed those people that died from hypothermia. Suddenly, I'm not sure he did. He should have appeared today."

After an hour, Hugh reached for the button to turn off the screens. He noticed movement.

"Were you expecting a visitor today, Dodge?"

Dodge looked.

"Well, look at those fellas. Bring the junkier car for the bullet holes. They didn't dress up either. What is all the gunk on the bottom of the car?"

45 Second Takedown

Liam looked at the monitor and grabbed a gun and ammunition off the wall. Dodge did the same and followed Liam. They ran into Hugh's backyard and through the gate.

Hugh threw a gun at Carter and next grabbed the ammunition.

"You know the fallback plan. This may be Simon with his men."

Hugh and Carter snuck across the street using the trees and bushes as cover. They moved closer to the street next to a neighbor's house. The front of the Dodge's house was in their view. They watched from the front arborvitae bush as Simon knocked on the house door. He looked very much like their doctored photo.

They saw Dodge without his gear open the door.

Carter whispered, "It's a good thing we put together some fake boxes."

"We're fine until Simon opens the box. Then all hell is going to break loose. Get ready."

Hugh smeared some black makeup on his and Carter's face.

"Camouflage is always a good idea."

"I think the guy threw two items in the bushes."

"Maybe they were garbage," suggested Carter.

Hugh looked worried.

"This group has occasionally used blowing devices to kill people. Anyway, the old group did. They were the worst group of criminals and targeted college students mostly for their recruits. I wouldn't trust a blowing device made by any one of them, a new person or old person."

"Their hands are hidden inside the car."

Hugh jabbed his arm at Carter.

"Ow, I was looking for missing fingers."

"Shh, they might hear you talking. The men have gloves."

Carter waited a full minute. He lowered his voice.

"I didn't see any gloves."

Hugh's face looked at him sarcastically.

"No one comes to buy illegal drone parts without gloves. They can't be stupid."

"I read the file about women. Cathy's body contained a lot of tattoos. She also showed a bite wound on her leg. The coroner mentioned shark. Liam was smart removing the women from this drill."

Hugh saw a hand on the screen door.

"Get ready, the man is coming outside."

Carter dropped the makeup tin when they heard shots coming from inside the house. They saw Simon run out onto the porch with his gun smoking.

"The little creep must have figured out this was a setup."

Carter and Hugh took a shot at the vehicle. Glass splintered. The back fender fell off. The driver spun out with Simon hanging onto the door. The man ran alongside the vehicle and jumped inside when

Dodge and Liam burst out the front door. Liam was in riot gear with black makeup. Dodge wore large sunglasses with a hippie shirt and torn jeans. He looked like a wild man with his long hair and beard.

They all ran for Dodge's truck. He squealed tires backing up, and the truck shot after the vehicle. Liam was on his cell calling for backup. They drove three blocks before they were close enough to shoot.

Liam yelled.

"Shoot now!"

Dodge drove erratically to avoid the bullets coming toward them from the front vehicle. He grabbed his bulletproof vest and put the vest on backward while driving.

Liam, Hugh, and Carter shot at the tires. Finally, the car flipped and rolled. The truck spun beyond the rolled car and swung around in front of the rolled-over vehicle. The men jumped out of the truck and handcuffed the men as they slowly tried to climb out of the vehicle which was smoking near the gas tank.

Carter grabbed the fire extinguisher and aimed at the smoke.

Dodge dragged the prisoners to his truck and used another handcuff to attach the men to a chain on the bumper. Once they were secure, Liam stepped over and looked at the men until he found the man he was looking for.

Simon was unconscious from the car crash.

Dodge looked at Liam.

"Do you think he broke anything?"

Liam bent down.

"He's still breathing. The perp probably rolled and bounced a little. There aren't any bones sticking out."

"Should we call the ambulance?"

"We probably should give the man the benefit of the doubt. He shouldn't die on us."

By the time the police and paddy truck arrived, Simon was moaning. He came to as Jonathan drove up.

"Nice job, men."

Liam pointed at Simon.

"Don't let this one get away."

"Simon Needham. You are alive. Imagine that. I thought you were a bigger man. I was wrong," said their Captain.

The ambulance people arrived and checked out the car passengers. None of them were seriously hurt.

"Officers, please take these scum bags away. Book them for trying to purchase military-grade drone parts, attempted murder, murder, and harassment towards my detectives."

Carter jabbed Hugh.

"They aren't wearing gloves."

Hugh congratulated Carter.

"You noticed. Bright was not the first thought for the day."

Carter wasn't sure what Hugh meant by the last statement. He decided to agree.

"Right."

There was an explosion that happened down the street where Dodge's house stood. The men watched as a large fireball appeared. The sky above the house was filled with black smoke. The wind carried the house pieces into a field next to the property. The weeds caught fire.

"I guess my new house plans might come in handy. I wonder who owns the lot next door," said Dodge.

Jonathan corrected himself.

"Add bombing a residential home, starting a fire, and pollution to the prisoners' charges."

The officer nodded, and the prisoners were placed inside the paddy wagon. Simon was double-chained.

"Sorry about your house, Dodge."

The five men stood and watched the smoke.

"My truck's fine. A few dings in the large front grille are all. I was smart and ordered the heavier truck. I probably can bang them dings out. A tiny rubber mallet works best. I've got the small jar of paint the dealership gave me. I shook the jar the other day, and the paint was still liquid."

The men stepped aside as the fire trucks drove around the two vehicles blocking the road. The school bus of kids was waiting.

"The tow truck has been called for this junk car. There's goose poop around the inside driver door. They must live on a farm. We'll find the place. See you in the office. You might want to take some days off with pay."

The detectives followed the firetrucks in Dodge's truck. He parked the truck in his favorite spot when visiting Hugh.

"Good thing we took the large porterhouse steaks out of the freezer this morning," said Hugh.

"Carter can peel the potatoes. Liam and I know how to make potato salad. I saw the new mayonnaise jar and pickles in the refrigerator in the garage. Emma has strawberries and an angel food cake in the freezer."

They watched for five minutes as the chimney tumbled.

"I'm going to miss the pink Christmas lights."

Liam and Hugh started laughing. Dodge joined in.

"It took a whole day to hang those lights."

Carter didn't get the joke.

The three men went back to Hugh's house. They put their riot gear in empty boxes in the garage to return to the office. The guns and ammunition also went into a box.

Carter watched the last house wall wiggle slightly and the fireman stood as the wall fell. He stared at the burn on the fence between the two houses. There was nothing but char. The fence collapsed, and the gate stood.

The mothers escorted their children home, and the school bus left.

Carter was glad they put in the gate. He went into the garage and deposited his gear. Carter hit the button to close the garage door.

Hugh was waiting for him.

"I need to apologize. They found gloves inside the junk car."

Carter believed Hugh could have kept the information to himself.

"I made the club today."

"You are totally in the club."

Hugh went inside. Carter went inside the house and washed his hands in the laundry room. He stepped into the noisy kitchen. A large pot of potatoes was waiting with the peeler.

"The gate is still standing."

The three men turned. Liam and Dodge stopped their meal preparations.

Hugh put the eggs on the stove and turned the burner to the on position. He went to a cupboard and grabbed a bottle. Liam was surprised at the label.

Hugh laughed.

"One of the drone manufacturers' sent me a gift. He likes the Mexican tequila Beeker imports."

Carter looked at their faces. He forgot about the black makeup.

"You men look terrible. We should wash this black soot and makeup off."

"We don't want the firemen to feel out of place," mentioned Hugh.

Carter started peeling the potatoes. Halfway through, Hugh finally found what he was looking for in the cupboard.

"There they are. Emma shoved them to the back. She forgets their importance on occasions such as this one."

He poured the liquid into four small shot glasses.

"Liam?"

Liam took the first shot glass.

"A toast to a successful mission today. Without my detectives, we wouldn't have captured a very horrible piece of humanity and his gang. Now the women can come home."

Dodge clapped loudly. The detectives clinked their glasses.

"Hear, hear," said Dodge.

Carter's eyes bulged and watered.

Dodge slapped him on the back.

"You'll learn. Beeker's tequila is well known."

Liam slipped away to call Penelope and give her a summary of the two takedowns.

"When you have your flight information tomorrow, text me."

"Don't party too much with the firemen. Let me correct my statement. Don't party too much with your detectives."

"I won't. Someone has to stay sane."

46 Final Case Wrap

More people from Simon's gang were arrested. His girlfriend was upset she stayed at the farmhouse. A few more people from the engineers' friends were found waiting for the drone parts in their garage. The fourth engineer was taken into custody at his home along with the awaiting buyer. The buyer carried a notebook of the prospective names of his customers on his computer.

All in all, the case criminals were many and from diverse backgrounds. There was some doubt as to who exactly killed four people and two security guards. Simon and his group were blamed. The loss of Dodge's house was worth the effort. No one missed the wallpaper.

The female detectives returned to the office. Davidson retired. Hugh, Penelope, and Carter were given a promotion. The detectives received bonuses. Dodge received a new landscape job courtesy of the department. His insurance paid for the removal and rebuild of his new home.

The court dates were far out into the future. The detectives settled down and fell into their normal routine.

One day Paul Beeker stopped by the office to congratulate Jonathan regarding the capture of the criminals that killed his wife. He acknowledged Jane's sister did get into a bad crowd. He expressed his disappointment Cathy was shot by one of Los Angeles's detectives. Jonathan told him the detectives had every right to shoot. He reminded Paul four of his detectives were wounded and one policeman died. Cathy continued firing at his detectives and didn't stop when commanded. Their only logical next step was to defend themselves. Paul mentioned his wife's sister wasn't exactly obedient at home either. Jonathan let Paul know the force was sorry for his loss. He told Paul he always admired how strong Jane Beeker appeared. He didn't use the word deadly. Cathy was the deadly one.

Liam and Penelope were out of the office surfing for the day in Laguna. Two people ran from the water.

The surfers planted their boards in the sand.

"I'm getting better, right?"

"Liam, you are surfing way better. Still, a few more lessons from a professional wouldn't hurt."

"You are a pro. Why don't you teach me?"

Penelope was pleased he grabbed her swimsuit and pulled her close.

"I would teach you, but you don't listen. You make excuses."

He kissed her.

"I'm listening to you now."

She pushed him away and grabbed her board.

"No, you're not."

He sighed and complained to a group of surfers who walked past.

"Why are women so difficult?"

The young surfers laughed. They knew Penelope.

"We're not responding Liam. You are on your own."

"Somewhere I've heard that before."

Liam took his surfboard and followed his wife to Dodge's truck. He was waiting for them.

"It's nice to watch the two of you fall off those toothpicks you flopped in the water. I never understood surfing amongst the critters."

Liam was impressed to see Dodge with his arm around Susan.

"I know. The ocean was a little busy with the young people trying to surf. I came close to several in the water. Since when did the two of you become good friends?"

Dodge blushed.

"One day he showed me his house that was being built. We walked through the rooms. I told him that I liked dogs and kids."

"She's a natural," beamed Dodge.

Penelope joined them.

"I'll drop your boards off at the beach house for you. I'll put them near the back patio."

"Thanks, Dodge, we'll catch the bus to our hotel."

47 Hotel and Rain

Penelope and Liam rode the bus to their hotel and went to their room. She looked at the throng of visitors walking the sidewalks. People were laughing and enjoying themselves.

Life should flow normally, and life did for other people. Because their jobs were different, they saw the uglier side. They did get to step away. The time was more precious whenever the detectives did.

Her husband looked at the greenery.

"This place is filled with sights, sounds, and smells."

She watched the tall palm trees.

"I'm glad we tried surfing further south. The water is much warmer near Laguna. This is our stop."

Liam took a quick shower. He held the door for Penelope.

"Need any help?"

"I can soap and rinse myself."

Liam dressed in casual slacks and a shirt. He waited on the patio. She dressed in a white cotton gauze outfit and joined him.

"I went to see a few houses around Dana Point yesterday."

Penelope took a small towel and dried her hair.

"Dana Point. Did we talk about a house?"

He watched as she took the large comb and did her hair. He handed her the pink hair tie. She put the hair length in the band.

"We can talk now. We agreed to a discussion when the case was over."

Penelope knew about their talk at the condominium.

"I'm not sure that I am ready for the house and the whole ball of wax."

Liam knew she was going to bail.

"All right. Six more months. You can think about things. I'm going to walk to the beach."

Penelope was left alone. She put her tennis shoes on, grabbed the room key, and two bottles of cold water. She went out of the hotel door. Liam was waiting for her.

"I hoped you would follow me."

He took the water bottle. They walked together on the upper sidewalk above the beach. The surf was pounding in the distance.

"The wind has picked up since we left."

"We stopped surfing at the correct time. This would be dangerous. There's so much spray that you can't see. Also, the undertow is too much."

They walked a mile.

"I didn't mean to put you off."

Liam thought about them.

"I know. My personality pushes."

Penelope stopped at a bench. Liam joined her. They opened their water bottles.

"I like the way things are between us. We have freedom and privacy. There's time for the job and time for us."

"You are afraid things might change."

She nodded.

"We can wait."

"You are sure?"

Liam took her fingers and rubbed them.

"I'm good."

Penelope put her head on his shoulder. They let the wind swirl around them. She noticed a dark cloud approaching.

"We should get to the hotel. The cloud looks ominous. I can smell the rain over the salt."

Liam couldn't smell anything.

"Why is the rain following us? Australia and now California."

They looked at the ocean as large water drops pelted them. He grabbed her hand, and they ran as hard as they could. By the time they reached the inside hotel doorway, they were completely drenched.

He pulled her close and kissed her.

"You look like a very wet wild woman."

He plucked a branch from her hair with a leaf attached. She noticed the rain stopped.

"Let's step outside and see if we can find a rainbow."

They went outside and walked to the sidewalk. Liam took her arm, and they continued in the opposite direction. There was little wind. They came around a bend.

"There is your rainbow. The colors are a little pale."

Penelope stood with Liam enjoying the view. Other couples joined them on the walkway. They let an elderly couple move ahead of them.

"They walk pretty briskly for their age."

"I think it's nice they jog together. We jog and hug."

Liam rubbed Penelope's back. She confessed.

"Susan's comment about dogs and kids got to me."

Penelope knew the comment bothered her husband as well.

"Do you think the two of them are serious?"

Liam shook his head.

"I don't know. Dodge has been quiet. I think Susan is frustrated with Carter."

Penelope watched the two young people when they were at work. There was a distance between them. They didn't fully connect.

"Dodge will be better for her."

They walked to their hotel and changed for dinner.

Liam dug into his fish.

"The lobster is delicious. We should buy the picture we saw at the gallery near Monterey."

Liam liked the large picture. The tree would be perfect for their den.

"We'll stop on our return and visit the aquarium. I'll make our hotel reservations. There are some fun restaurants and shops in the area."

Penelope cut her steak. She passed her fork so he could try the meat.

"Wow. The flavor is good. I should ask the chef where he buys his meat, and what spices he uses. Hugh would keel over with jealousy if I can reproduce this taste in a steak."

She smiled and raised her eyebrows. The spice jars were in her suitcase. The chef sold the jar through the gift shop. She purchased jars for their friends. Liam noticed.

"You are smiling at me a little too assured of yourself."

"I have a gift in our room."

Liam paused.

"No."

"Yes, I asked the chef."

"Get out. He gave you the recipe."

She chuckled.

"Not quite, but the ingredients are listed on the jar."

Liam was joyous.

"How many jars?"

The waiters took away their plates.

"Check, please."

"Enough jars for everyone. We can always come back and buy more. This place has good vibes for us."

Suddenly her husband was in a hurry to return to their room.

48 New Development

Jonathan called Liam into his office.

"Captain, what's up?"

"My wife and I went to a party at Paul Beeker's mansion. We did have a good time. The food was great, the music was for the older crowd, and the guests were many people I haven't seen for some time."

His lead detective developed a stony look on his face.

"Look, Liam, the Chief, and his wife were invited. They are in Bermuda. I was relegated to represent them at Beeker's party. The job always comes first. There is a new development."

The lead detective believed Jonathan was coming to his point.

"Paul has a fiancée. We know Jane died eight months ago. The man has moved fast. I thought he might wait considering what happened to her. Investigation of his company hasn't slowed him at all. The whole evening was a shocker."

Liam was paying attention.

"What news shocked you and the guests?"

"We all hoped he would take some time and work on the holes in his business. His lawyer didn't look exactly happy about the proposal and the possible marriage. His expression gave him away."

Liam saw the cursed look on the lawyer's face at the Long Beach warehouse after their first bombed-out raid.

"The lawyer won't bless the union. He doesn't want Paul to remarry. Without a wife, Paul is more valuable. A wife brings complications. I'm not offended in the least."

Jonathan toyed with his ink pen.

"I think Beeker might have more trouble than he bargained for with this woman. She is strongminded."

Now Liam's curiosity rose even higher.

"Who exactly is this woman?"

Jonathan tapped his pen on his desk pad. There was no neat way of breaking the news. The announcement might appear any day in the newspapers.

"She's a designer. The woman is someone you know."

Jonathan stopped tapping. The room was quiet. Liam looked at the ceiling. His suspicion about who was Paul Beeker's next leading lady couldn't be true.

"You are wrong."

Jonathan dropped his pen.

"She was there holding his hand."

Liam faltered. He couldn't believe his boss. There was pain on his face. He hadn't talked with the person in a long time.

"I should talk with her."

Jonathan disagreed.

"Becka Smith is no longer your responsibility. You married Penelope King instead of her. I doubt she considers your opinion important or of any value."

Liam didn't know how to respond. Jonathan picked up his pen.

"The reason we need to talk is more than the Beeker party. There is some other information that has been discovered."

Liam knew the men in prison were being interviewed.

"Per one of the prisoners, Paul Beeker's father belonged to the gang in his youth. This is the reason Simon targeted Cathy. We think he pursued her to join. He indoctrinated her into the gang and their ways. Jane tried to intervene and was unsuccessful. James Beeker left the gang on his own in his twenties. According to gang rules, no one leaves."

"We thought they disbanded. What are you saying? We may not have caught all the members of this original gang, and there could be repercussions in the future because of Beeker's father?"

Jonathan showed him a paper birth certificate. Liam looked at the document.

"The original gang is more than likely in a nursing home or dead. The original gang did write a book which is out of print. This book could have found its way into their hands. Here's the other discovery. Simon Needham has a stepbrother. We've tried to find him. Simon also claims his people didn't kill the four or the guards at the warehouse. We don't believe him."

Liam knew the focus was now off Paul Beeker and his fiancée. He was afraid to ask.

"This stepbrother owned a red helicopter at one time."

Jonathan knew Liam was a step ahead of him.

"The stepbrother was flying the red helicopter at warehouse one. Simon was never near the warehouse nor the airfield where Cathy met her end. He was safe offsite. The stepbrother might have been the brains of the drone operation."

Jonathan showed him a photograph of the stepbrother named Steve Neely.

"We believe Simon was safely tucked away at the farmhouse waiting for their call."

"The two men look alike," commented Liam.

"The man disappeared a few days before we arrested Simon. Our investigators talked with his mother. The two men shared the same father. She kept her name. The stepbrother more than likely is in Oregon. We're not sure, but we've notified the police."

Liam rubbed his hand through his hair.

"I still need to warn Becka. Paul is not a good choice. She loves her parents very much and is super protective of them. She will drop Paul."

Jonathan saw the lights blinking on his intercom. His calls were on hold with his secretary. The intercom came on.

"The chief is on line 2."

"Tell him I will call him back in five minutes."

Jonathan put the photograph in the file folder.

"I still disagree with your talking with Ms. Smith. I have a good detective in my workforce, and I don't want her focus to drop. She's brave and headstrong which are qualities the force needs. The woman stands her ground. Those are the major reasons she was hired. I hope I'm making myself extremely clear."

"Is that an order?"

Jonathan was older and wiser.

"You are free to make the call. My recommendation has been given. I'll step aside."

Liam left his boss's office. He went into his own office. Finally, he went outside to the parking ramp and made a phone call.

"Becka, we need to talk. Meet me."

Liam grabbed his jacket and disappeared. He forgot about his lunch date with Penelope.

49 Consequences

The deli was full. Penelope grabbed two barstools in the corner. She sat waiting at the deli and finally ordered her veggie sandwich. Penelope called Hugh. She put her hand over her other ear to drown out the noise.

"Have you seen Liam?"

Hugh did see Liam through a restaurant window when he stopped at a light. At the time he continued down the street. Hugh tapped on his horn a few times.

"I've got to stop. My horn is going berserk. This is the same car with the air conditioner problem."

Penelope remembered the car. She returned to the office. She saw Jonathan wasn't busy.

"Hi, I think I've lost Liam. He didn't show for lunch. His schedule doesn't show out of the office. Hugh used the horn trick on me. Is there something strange that I might have missed?"

"Sit down, Penelope. We do have a vehicle that will be replaced soon. The horn might have failed. The lighter stopped working, and the outside mirror fell off. I'm glad you checked with me. There has been a new development in our recent case. Now that you are here, I can share."

He informed her about Simon's stepbrother and the information they obtained.

"I'll post the information for the other detectives. They need to be made aware of the man. He was more than likely their gang's recruiter. Without any money from Cathy's parents, he might have moved elsewhere. We can only hope he is gone from Los Angeles."

Jonathan put his ink pen down.

The intercom came on. Jonathan's secretary was persistent.

"The District Attorney is on line one."

"I'm sorry. This call is one that mustn't be ignored."

"Of course, the DA is important."

Penelope removed herself, so Jonathan could visit. He cupped his hand over his phone.

"Penelope, come to this office any time. All my detective's opinions matter. I was impressed with you when we first met. I'm still impressed," said Jonathan.

"I will. Thank you."

She ran into Liam outside the building. He mechanically kissed her and turned to go inside.

"Liam?"

He looked at her face. She looked accusingly at him. Liam realized the reason for her look.

"Lunch was today with you at the deli. I forgot. I'm sorry."

Penelope watched him disappear. She walked to her sports car. She drove toward the beach house. At the turn westward, she continued driving on the freeway. She reached the condominium parking lot. She sat in her car.

"Something is wrong."

She turned around and looked at her gas gauge. Penelope filled the tank with gas. She drove home to the beach house. Liam's car was in the garage.

"Where were you? You left before I did."

"I drove to the condominium."

Liam frowned.

"You are upset about my missing lunch. Something came up."

"I'm upset that people avoided me. You were one of them. Your boss was super nice. People might have seen you at lunch today. I'm sure Hugh did. He wouldn't give me an answer."

Liam was caught. He wasn't sure if anyone saw him and Becka at the restaurant. He didn't know. Hugh would deflect for him, but not for long. He decided to play it safe.

"Becka is dating Paul Beeker. I ate lunch with her. I warned her about Paul's father. He used to belong to the gang in his youth."

Penelope now got the full picture. Her husband ate lunch with a former girlfriend. The lunch was no accident. The lunch was personal.

"I'm not hungry."

She took a wine bottle, a glass, and the opener outside on the patio. She sat down at a chair near the table.

Liam brought a wine glass outside. He pulled a chair closer to her. She slid her chair away from him. He grabbed the bottle off the table and opened the wine. He handed her the filled glass.

"I did tell you I was sorry about missing lunch."

Penelope didn't talk. They sat in silence. He should explain.

"Her parents are important to her. She needed access to information about the Beeker's. Jonathan disagreed, but he let me decide. I know Becka. She would want me to tell her."

"Why didn't you call me?"

Liam drank his wine.

"You would have reacted badly like how you are behaving now. Becka upsets you."

She was more upset by his statement.

"Wrong, my husband upset me royally. I'm driving to the condominium."

Liam let her go.

"Headstrong is a mild term."

He figured she would calm down in a day or two. She stayed for five days at their condominium before he drove there to see his wife.

She heard him in the kitchen. He hated her being gone. He did what he needed to do about Becka. He rationalized his disclosure to his former girlfriend was professionally motivated. Penelope thought the disclosure was personal.

Liam held her.

"Pink, we're on the same team. Give me a chance and trust me. I would do the same for you. I missed you so much."

He hadn't called her Pink for a long time. Sweet memories flooded her. A silver frame was handed to him. The picture inside was of the two of them at their wedding. He put the picture on the counter relieved at the good timing of the photograph's arrival. She held onto him.

Liam breathed a sigh of relief. She told him that she missed him, too. He smelled her hair and held on. There was only one woman he wanted.

He acknowledged his boss was wiser. Liam would try harder.

"Will you teach me more surfing lessons tomorrow."

"Sure, we can do turnarounds at the beach house beach if the waves aren't too bad in the area."

Liam avoided turnarounds in the past.

"Turnarounds will be interesting. Jump the rope before it trips you."

"No jumping."

"I want to do turnarounds here. This is your beach. I threw our wet suits in my trunk."

Penelope was pleased he remembered the suits.

"This is our beach. The water is cool."

Liam was relieved.

"I should have called about lunch with Becka."

"You will in the future," reminded Penelope.

For Liam, the consequences were too painful.

"Yes, ma'am."

50 House Party

Liam escorted Penelope to Dodge's front door. Dodge held the door wide open. The house was lit from within and without. The exterior lights were focused to enhance the modern design.

The helicopter was hidden by a decorative wall and plants from the street. A person driving by would never see the beautiful bird.

"Penelope, you look amazing in your dress. Pink flowers are always nice in a sundress. I don't know what they call that fabric, but the soft shine matches your eyes."

She gave Dodge a quick kiss.

"The woman is smelling nice, too."

"I'm glad you cut your hair and shaved. The new black outfit helps."

Dodge pulled her closer. Liam intervened.

"Go find your own broad, Dodge. This one is taken."

Susan squealed with delight at seeing the Knight couple.

"Come in. We have furniture. No chintz allowed. Leather stuff wears better."

Penelope and Susan disappeared into the kitchen where the other women congregated. Liam stayed and talked with Dodge.

"How did you get the Homeowner's Association to approve the helicopter pad?"

Dodge chuckled.

"I purchased the lot under a different corporation name. The lot isn't part of this complex. They couldn't connect the dots. The county approved the helipad."

Hugh joined them in a brightly colored shirt and a lei. He put a red plastic lei around Liam's neck.

"You are part of the red team. We're playing games later."

Liam groaned. He hated party games.

"My thoughts are running down the same street. At least he didn't buy the grass skirts. I was hoping you could come up with a plan to squash the games. The bomb already happened. We shouldn't use that ploy again."

Liam saw his friend was in an exceptionally great frame of mind this evening.

"We should ask Carter for any ideas."

Dodge shook his head.

"He bowed out of the party. He called a couple of minutes ago."

Liam didn't know Carter was having difficulty with Dodge dating Susan.

"I saw his car down the street. He was sitting inside. I thought he got lost. He hasn't shown?"

Dodge disappeared and returned with Hugh.

"We need to bring him here. Susan's requested we drag him out of the car if necessary. She won't take no for an answer. I can't blame her. This is her first big party. We're supposed to have fun this evening or else."

The three detectives surrounded Carter's car. They rocked the car fender. Carter stepped out.

"Where are the police when you need them? My running into detectives from Los Angeles on such a pretty evening wasn't expected."

Hugh moved forward. Carter stepped away from the car door.

"Cut the crap, Carter. You are coming to Susan's party. She bought lots of vegetables and stuff per Emma. Her hard-earned money isn't going to be wasted. You are going to appear sociable. By the way, what is your first name?"

"Cantor. I hate my first name. People made fun of my name when I was a kid."

Dodge gently shoved Carter aside.

"Cantor isn't so bad. I've heard worse. Horses canter or trot. I forget which."

Dodge took the car out of the park position. The three men shoved the car down the street toward Dodge's house. Carter stalled. The men were okay with his name. He ran to help them roll his car to the curb.

"I should turn the car around."

"You can leave the car where it is and join the party. We're playing games. There's water involved. I made sure the hot water was turned on. The temperature should be medium."

Carter groaned.

"Whose bright idea was the games?"

Hugh looked at him evilly.

"Right, games for the kids. We need to show them how to have fun. I get the role model concept."

The four men returned to the house. The competition in the backyard became heated when the ball toss dunked a person. The dunking game became a game of war. The kids watched from the open bedroom window and pointed.

After the men were all wet, The women handed out the prizes. Inside the packages were a dry pair of sweat clothes.

The men changed and put burgers on the grill. Liam looked at one of the pale patties and smelled.

"What is this stuff? Chicken meat or tuna?"

Hugh looked at one of the burgers.

"Old meat for sure."

Dodge came over and looked.

"Susan purchased some turkey and veggie burgers. They do smell strange like cooked zucchini."

Liam quickly put the burgers on a separate plate. Hugh took the flipper and helped separate the burgers from real meat.

"There, I've fixed the platters."

Carter handed Hugh two trays of buns. Hugh took the platters over to the light.

"Pumpernickel and wheat with the white sesame seed bakery buns is a no-no."

He separated the buns and handed Carter the platters.

Dodge tossed a jar to Hugh. Hugh's eyes bulged.

"No way. I'll be right back."

Liam looked at the jar. He picked the jar up and held it to the light.

"Where on earth did you find this product?"

"Isn't this cool? They put a mustard strip, a ketchup strip, a pickle strip, a horseradish strip, and sliced jalapenos in one jar," said Dodge happily.

Hugh returned with his plastic jar of mustard. There was a label on the outside.

"Back off, Hugh's mustard."

Penelope saw the men and the jar. She refrained from smiling. Liam handed her the odd buns and weird patties.

"We'll get the kids and dogs to eat first with Susan. Leave the water tank when you are done. The kids want to give the game a try."

Liam moved the real meat burgers off to the warming tray. Hugh felt guilty at being a bad guest when one of the kids used a swear word that was his favorite.

"I like the thousand island dressing Susan bought and the lettuce salad. Excuse me for a minute. The kids need a referee."

Hugh ran out to the yard to shush the language and came inside again. Carter joined the approval party.

"The salad sure looked great. There were yellow pickled banana peppers. I prefer jalapenos. They are hotter."

Liam looked at Dodge.

Dodge handed Hugh a tiny jar of sweet pickles when he came inside.

"We wanted to let you know you won the ducking contest."

"Gee, thanks, guys. Ant magnets."

He opened the jar and threw them out to the dogs who jumped high in the air.

Carter couldn't contain himself anymore.

"You are all crazy. I'm going to the kitchen where things are less dangerous. I'm eating some carrots and celery."

Liam looked at Hugh.

Hugh whispered.

"The cans are tied to Carter's back bumper. I had a hard time finding the large cans at the store the other day. Most of them are plastic. Oh, I painted them glow-in-the-dark colors. The cans are tucked under the car."

Penelope returned.

"Our turn to eat."

Liam took the real meat burgers off the grill. Hugh carried the buns inside. The three detectives joined the women. The kids and dogs ran around outside playing hide and seek.

After dinner, Emma took the kids and dog home. Their maid was staying overnight to care for the kids. Dodge put his dog in the house in the master bedroom. He dumped the intact feather pillow on the couch.

"Feathers are the dog's newest fascination. We have to hide them."

The men went outside and shot fireworks while the women cleaned up.

Emma returned as did the men. They congregated around the front porch drinking coffee. Finally, Carter stood to leave. They watched him get in his vehicle, turn the engine on, and he pulled away from the curb. The cans made a loud racket.

Carter drove in figure eight in front of Dodge's house. The onlookers cheered. He waved on the second round and drove away.

Penelope, Liam, Emma, and Hugh said their goodnights.

51 Ride and Home

Liam handled his black sports car around a curve and missed the stacked cans on the side of the road.

"Carter removed the neon cans. I'm glad Hugh painted them."

"The party was nice. You didn't mind the games too much?"

"The games were fun. Carter figured out we rigged the dunking machine. He found the block of wood we inserted so the chair wouldn't fall in the water when we were on the base. I liked the bowling game the best. The dogs ran away with the ball. I counted ten balls in the yard when we went inside to eat. Nine of them had holes in them. A few of the pins were missing. They probably are in the garden with the pickles."

Penelope remembered the fun look on Hugh's children's faces.

"Do you still have the realtor's card for Dana Point?"

Liam put the card on his desk at home.

"The lot next to Dodge is available. We could build."

"We are more beachy-type people. Carter told me he was going to buy a boat with his bonus and promotion money. We might have fun parties playing volleyball on the beach and swimming to an anchored boat."

"The realtor's card is at the beach house. Did he say what kind of boat?"

"Sailboat, I think."

Liam wondered about the sailboat.

"We might all want to purchase a sailboat together or a motorboat. The boat would be larger, and we could store her in a marina. A boat might allow us more freedom. There are no bears around the ocean in these waters."

She thought about the other sea creatures. Penelope looked at her husband.

"Becka called me today."

Liam turned onto the freeway. He squeezed her hand.

"She wanted to thank me for letting you warn her. Becka has broken their engagement and dropped Paul Beeker. She gave his ring back. An attorney friend is her current focus. Becka raved about him. He lives in Greece."

Liam knew the man.

He lifted her hand and kissed her fingers. Liam was happy. He pressed her fingers to his heart. Penelope was thinking about buying a house. She would come around to their plan. He would give her the space she required.

"Jonathan will be pleased. He was worried about Becka, too. You see he enjoyed talking with her whenever she visited the office."

"Our boss likes women."

"Tell me about it. He wanted to fire me if you left the detective force and just recently. I'm glad you stayed."

Penelope was glad Liam came to his senses. She thought about children.

"I still need some more time on the other subject."

"Understood," said Liam.

He turned into their condominium. She looked puzzled.

"I missed the turn."

Penelope liked surfing at their condominium when she wasn't being a detective.

"Come on, wife. I'm tired. We have the whole weekend to play."

He opened her door. The Knight couple went inside their condominium building. Liam waved to the security guard.

Unlocking their door, he pulled her inside.

Liam kissed her passionately in the moonlight. Penelope believed there was much more to life than work or worrying about ex-persons. She briefly thought about their next case that came across her desk about the man who used bombs. He used them against any people or any strange cause he didn't like.

He felt her disappear. Liam read the same case file. He shouldn't have sent her the file. Tomorrow could stay put. Bombs were off the table. Liam tried a different tactic. Penelope responded.

"I'm here."

"It's hard to make love alone."

"Count on me joining in."

"Good."

Liam picked up his wife. The moonlight seemed brighter. The stars peeked out. The night was made for love and music.

"Did your mom send you the new dress?"

Penelope couldn't resist.

"I opened a charge account at the high-end store. They gave me twenty percent off."

Liam dropped her immediately.

"Not to worry, I received a promotion. I splurged on the dress. Dodge noticed."

"I noticed the pink magnolia dress. I wanted to leave the party before we arrived."

Liam picked the remote and turned to one song on their recorder.

"Don't tell me the price."

She slid until her feet touched his.

"Remember this song?"

Penelope did. Liam twirled her in their bare feet in their living room. He started singing the song he played on the radio in their first car ride together on the Los Angeles detective force. She joined him in the chorus. They sang in harmony. The two danced to the music in perfect rhythm.

A slow dance came on next.

"This one is better."

She and Liam fit. There were no more words spoken. The beautiful night belonged to them. Liam stopped and pulled the drapes shut. Penelope was ahead of him.

Some things were private.

52 Interview with Simon, Only the Joker

Liam waited calmly as the jailor escorted Simon Needham into the room.

Liam told him his name and his job with the Los Angeles detective force.

Simon snorted.

"You were the dude in armor firing toward my car. I was just trying to make a living, and you shot my car to heck and back."

"I was involved in the concealment plan to find illegal drone part buyers. You fell for the bait."

The prisoner laughed.

"I destroyed your house."

"You destroyed a house with terrible wallpaper. The house wasn't mine. Let's not go down that old road. Tell me about your stepbrother."

Simon suddenly knew the police might know about his relationship and where the chopper was hidden.

"I don't know what you are talking about."

Liam slid the picture of the red helicopter and the copy of the birth certificate across to the prisoner.

The prisoner examined the paper on the backside.

"These pages are blank."

Liam was losing his patience.

"You will go down for killing those people in the warehouse."

Simon hesitated.

"My lawyer told me yesterday. You are going to have to prove I killed those people. I tell you that I wasn't there."

Liam lied.

"We have enough evidence."

Simon thought about who killed Cathy.

"My stepbrother knows about your wife. Detective Penelope Knight is her name. Maybe you should go home and wait for him to arrive. She killed his fiancée, Cathy. Someone has to pay were his last words to me."

Liam didn't react. He doubted Cathy was engaged to anyone at the time of her death.

"When you want to talk to me and disclose the truth regarding this case, your lawyer knows where my office is located. The deal I was going to offer has dropped a few notches, like six feet under. Oh, we thought you were one of the four dead people found in a warehouse. Weren't we surprised to find the joker was alive? The others on the tour died of hypothermia. Somebody froze them to death probably in a container or freezer."

"You aren't listening. I didn't kill those people. I changed my mind about the tour. I'm innocent."

Liam stretched his arms.

"I guess you were luckier than the other people. But here you are in jail behind heavy bars taking the heat for an absent leader. From where I'm standing, your luck just ran out. Be careful when you are outside in the prison yard. I hear drones have gun barrels on them now. Real bullets, too. One tiny bullet might not make a dent. Ten probably will do the job. There also is Jason to worry about. You remember Jason. He told us Steve was better at making bombs. We wondered about Steve. He's like the king leader in your game. Jason's confession was interesting. He said you forced him to join the buy-the-illegal-drone scheme and to make bombs that weren't up to par. He also fixed the car battery in the junk car. I guess he got tired of doing all the work around the good old farmhouse. Then there's your girlfriend."

Liam nodded to the guard. He liked pitting people against each other. The prisoner was taken away.

Liam contacted his boss.

"We have a real problem."

Liam drove home in a daze and missed the exit to the beach house. He turned around at the next exit. When he arrived home, he changed clothes, wrote his wife a note, and jogged to the beach.

Penelope joined him an hour later.

"Hey."

He responded, "Hey you are back."

"I take it the interview didn't go well."

"Steve Neely knows you shot his fiancée."

Penelope looked at the shore. The ocean moved no matter what transpired. The tide rolled in and out. Ships transported goods.

"We talked about this scenario as a possibility."

Liam reached for her hand.

"I was jolted. I should have sent Hugh and Carter to handle the interview. I might have blown things wide apart."

What did your boss tell you?"

Liam saw the sun dip.

"There she goes."

They watched as the sun removed itself from the horizon.

"He told me to go home and hug my wife."

Penelope smiled.

"Good advice. We have a great life. The beach house is waiting. I'll race you to the front door."

Liam didn't want to run. She ran a few paces and stopped.

53 Pre-Anniversary Gift and Their Future

Liam knew they would work the next cases together. Penelope was already onboard.

He joined her. They walked to the house from the beach. He waved his arms excitedly and talked. She was surprised by his enthusiasm.

"A guy called me about this huge ship. It needs some work."

Penelope was impressed.

"I thought we were looking for a medium-sized boat."

Liam kept chattering.

"This ship is a real steal. We need to make some modifications and fix the engine. A little bottom paint might be a good idea. Modern kitchen, new staterooms, fix the bridge windshield, and we'll be all set."

"What happened to the windshield?" asked Penelope.

"You don't want to know."

She could only guess the ship might have belonged to a drug runner. He saw her frown.

They reached their front door. His wife thought about a new house.

"Let's sit on the steps and talk. The house thing bothers me, too. We should be more North. I was thinking Malibu, or the surrounding area is closer to the office. There are nice hospitals in case we need one. Someday we will. Good fish restaurants are around the area."

"Your dad wasn't excited about ocean fish."

Her husband stopped talking about the large ship.

"Let me think about the Malibu area for a house."

"Understood."

Penelope opened their mailbox and sorted the few items in her hand. She handed him a card.

"Your mom and dad sent us an anniversary card. Our anniversary is three months away."

They went inside the beach house. He opened the card. Liam was astounded.

"You knew about this gift?"

She glanced at the card.

"My dad figured we would make the six-month mark. My mom bet on nine months."

Liam asked.

"What was your bet?"

She kissed her husband sweetly.

"You don't remember. I do. Note the heavy emphasis on I do."

"The *I-do-thing* was at the wedding. The vows were forever. Good. That's settled. We own five thousand acres in Montana. What do we do with the property?"

"We do own land and some buffalo."

Liam was stumped.

"How many buffalo, Penelope?"

She contemplated.

"The last time our foreman counted, there were fifty-eight."

Liam took her in his arms.

"Any lakes on our property?"

Penelope was way ahead of her husband.

"Two are big enough for a floatplane. My dad stocks the lake with fish each year."

Liam slowly decided where they should build a house. He grinned.

"No, no, not Montana. I left."

"I promised your dad I would keep you in a life which you were accustomed to. He's trying to help."

Penelope needed to correct her husband's thinking.

"I know flowers and money aren't your things."

Penelope was distressed.

"Hey, I get you are my rich girl. People who don't have a lot would disagree with your philosophy."

Liam was thinking small and rustic. He acknowledged they did have a great life in California. The Montana landscape filled his thoughts. He didn't know too much about bison. Fishing was a different story. No neighbors for miles drove his next conversation with his wife. Privacy up the wazoo would be an awesome concept.

"We could skip the large ship and Malibu house. We have lots of time for that stuff later."

His wife sighed.

"Liam, you are so wrong. Rich isn't where we go. One tiny fishing cabin will be allowed."

"And one small boat would seal the deal."

Liam knew his wife. She didn't consider herself rich. His wife pictured the cabin near the lake with a small boat. He would be okay with a smaller cabin to start. The scene in his mind was peaceful and serene.

The sun looked different in the Montana sky. The summers were always the best. Vacations in the North country would work for the Knights. They could get away from the city's heat and her problems.

His eyes gave him away. They were bright with happiness and hope. Liam wanted this dream to come true. He was letting her make the decision.

She would go along. They were partners in everything. There was also the other stuff she kept putting off. There would be children in their future eventually when she was ready.

Penelope took his large hands in hers. His were rough, and hers were smooth. She nodded her approval.

Liam jumped for joy. He was grateful.

"We have to celebrate. This is going to be fun. I'll call the architect's name your father sent me in an email."

"Did I tell you how sweet you look when you are excited? This is a conspiracy that I will overlook. I can't believe my father sent you an email. He doesn't know how to do email. No more."

He kissed her.

"Did I tell you how gorgeous you look?"

"Only ten times."

"You look gorgeous one more time."

"Flattery will get you more fun," said Penelope.

It was Liam's turn to relent.

"I certainly hope so."

Penelope pointed to the brochure on the table.

"My parents sent another gift."

Liam opened the brochure.

"Tickets are inside to a boat show in Montana. This is way cool. They also sent us airline tickets. How did they know my schedule?"

She was glad her parents called her.

"I have spies."

She handed him a second brochure. This one he read.

"They make log cabins in larger sizes."

Penelope knew the brochure was a mistake.

"My father has a stuffed bison head we can mount somewhere. The head was from the former owner of the herd who has retired. My dad has already ordered the antler chandelier for the entryway. My mom is searching for candlestick holders."

Liam was way ahead of her.

"Hugh. We can use the head. He feared the bear cubs. This is going to be good."

"Be gentle."

Liam held his gorgeous wife. He could be gentle. He knew Penelope was right. They could set up a photoshoot with the buffalo head for Hugh to send to his kids.

"An antler chandelier might be nice. Which cabin did your father recommend?"

Penelope knew her husband didn't see the penciled star on the brochure.

"We can talk later."

Liam could talk later. Other things were more important. The man tried his normally convincing moves. Penelope wasn't biting. He looked at his wife, and she was distant.

"Okay, what gives? You aren't telling me the facts you know about the area."

Penelope knew her husband. Her hesitation was obvious.

"There is an old airstrip five miles away. My dad told me the runway was in bad shape."

"Is the runway repairable?"

She didn't want to answer. Her husband would see the strip when he used his GPS. The airstrip was long with a couple of metal buildings.

"I haven't been to the area in years. The runway was hardpacked earth originally. Then the owner put tar on top. Jake Silverton was quite the character. He owned several airplanes before his death. He brought in the mail, food, supplies, and medicine for the locals. I imagine the tar can be resurfaced, and the gas tank replaced."

Liam breathed.

"Who owns the land today?"

The land was part of the ranch. Her father purchased any land that came up for sale adjacent to his properties.

"My dad loves the land. He is trying to save the universe or at least part of Montana. He and my mom purchased the land approximately five years ago. The metal buildings were emptied and repaired. He stores hay in them and farm equipment. They planted some evergreen trees to buffer the wind. Each year they cut a tree for Christmas and plant ten more."

"Imagine the possibilities. A real runway and a lake for floatplanes. Then there are the Christmas trees. The place sounds magical."

His wife knew if they repaired the runway, things would change. She didn't want things to change. Plus, the cost would be expensive.

"Liam."

He focused on his wife.

"I'm pushing too much. My fault when I get excited. This discussion changed my focus. I warned you before we got married."

She nodded.

Liam tossed the brochures. They hit the kitchen island and slid to a stop.

"One tiny fishing cabin with an antler chandelier will be fine. He said the chandelier was maybe three feet in width. My dad was rechecking the measurements."

Penelope was delighted her husband was back in focus. She kissed him longingly.

"You forgot about the boat."

She knew he was hopeless.

"I didn't forget the boat. We have a boat show."

Liam kissed his wife passionately. Things were always up for more discussion. He knew the antler chandelier was more like four feet in width. He deleted the email from Warren.

"I'm glad we settled everything."

Penelope closed her eyes. Liam knew the morning would come. His wife would be there in his arms. A man couldn't want anything more. Right now, he didn't need food.

One woman was the game plan. He was glad the cards were currently stacked in his favor. He could see the stars appear over their cabin and disappear in the morning. Liam was going to proceed very carefully on building this cabin.

"The master bedroom should be oriented, so we can see the sky in the morning. A pink sky would be preferred while I make us our coffee. But for now, there is only this moment with my gorgeous wife."

"You are a sweet, dangerous romantic."

Liam was sure he was.

"Every time."

LINDA MCKOWN

Author's List of Books

Knight Detective Series:
Book 1 - Gray Area for a Woman
Book 2 – Pink Sky in the Morning

Orange Carousel and Orchid Murders

Black Horse and Female Lawyer

Green Emeralds and Heist Club

White Boom and the Seagulls

Gold and the Spotted Jaguar

Raiment Red and a Raven
- A Southwest Mystery

A Wright Series:
Book 1 – Diamonds Blondes and Poison
Book 2 – Dead On Coordinates
Book 3 – Wild Golden Obsession
Book 4 – No Easy Target
Book 5 – Powerhouse Race
Book 6 – Cross Paths

www.ingramcontent.com/pod-product-compliance
Lightning Source LLC
La Vergne TN
LVHW020537100826
845148LV00010B/1497

* 9 7 8 1 7 3 4 4 0 9 5 4 3 *